Advance Praise:

"*The Pleasuring of Men* is the coming-of-age story of Tom Vaughan, a gay man living in New York City in the nineteenth century. It's his coming out story, the tale of his sexual blossoming as Tom works as a prostitute for an escort service thinly disguised as a messenger company called Young America. In the process, Tom learns about himself, his body, and humanity.

The novel is deftly drawn with rich descriptions, a rhythmic balance of action, dialogue, and exposition, and a nicely understated plot. *The Pleasuring of Men* is both engaging and provocative."

—Sean Moran

The Pleasuring of Men

Clifford Browder

Arlington, Virginia

Published by Gival Press, an imprint of Gival Press, LLC.

For information please write
Gival Press, LLC
P. O. Box 3812,
Arlington, VA 22203
www.givalpress.com

First edition
ISBN 978-1-92-8589-59-4
eISBN 978-1-92-8589-65-5
Library of Congress Control Number: 2011925413

Cover: Copyright by CURAphotography.
Design by Ken Schellenberg.

1

WHEN MR. NEIL SMYTHE became a roomer in our brownstone, my brother Stewart scowled and wondered if the subtle scent he gave off was cologne or "hair slime"; my mother declared his last name "elegant, and so much nicer than Smith"; and I said nothing, knowing that I'd just met the handsomest man in the world.

That we were taking in a roomer was the result of a desperate need to put our finances in order. Since my father's death years before, following his heavy losses in a panic, my mother, having mourned him interminably, through skimping and saving had done her best to maintain herself and her two sons in our handsome brownstone on Twenty-fifth Street just off the Fifth Avenue, a fashionable address that she could not bring herself to leave in a move to humbler quarters.

In matters of economy, alas, Mother's best was none too good. My father's older sister Jessie had descended upon us like a whirlwind, and having demanded to see Mother's account books, after a quick glance had pronounced them chaotic and illegible. At her insistence Stewart took charge of the books, and at his insistence Mother sold her carriage, implemented further economies, and put an ad in the paper for a roomer. Of the various responses, one on gilt-edged satin paper stood out, so Mother insisted that we interview this gentleman first. And Neil Smythe entered our lives.

A clean-shaven young man of twenty-two, he was tall and thin, with smooth skin and wavy long blond hair. He came to us correctly dressed in a gray frock coat, fawn trousers, and black pointed shoes, with a scarf pin and cufflinks that glittered, and a boyish look that I, myself sixteen, found stupendously appealing. While the interview proceeded in the parlor, Stewart and I waited in the sitting room. When Mother, having shown Mr. Smythe out, informed us that she had offered him the room and he had taken it, I was delighted.

Mr. Smythe soon moved in. It happened while I was at school, so I had no opportunity to view him and his belongings in the process. But from then on – at some cost to my studies at Dr. Murdock's Academy for Boys – I made it my chief occupation to observe our roomer discreetly and guess what kind of life he was leading. Because he was, so Mother informed us, a gentleman of independent means, he had the luxury of rising late and performing his ablutions at leisure, before going out for a late breakfast and errands, or whatever he might be up to. His room was on the third floor next to mine, so through the thick wall I could faintly hear him stirring, but little else. Occasionally I saw him in the hall, going to or from the bathroom in a green-silk dressing gown, ankle-length; he would nod civilly and hurry on, leaving me to savor in the air a hint of cologne or pomade. And in the bathroom I once found a pair of slippers he had left there, black velvet lined with blue silk: slippers such as I had never seen in my life. Hoping for a glimpse of him in his room, I knocked on his door and, when he opened it a crack, returned them to him. "Thank you, Tom," he said, took the slippers, and shut the door. He wasn't easy to know.

When he went out by day, he wore a brown derby, a tan frock coat with a velvet collar and lapels, checked or pinstriped trousers, a yellow waistcoat with a shimmering watch chain across it, a red or green silk cravat, black shoes with pointed toes, and a tasseled walking stick, all in the very height of fashion. I envied him hugely, having lived in my brother's hand-me-downs for years, only rarely getting clothes of my own. Usually he returned in the late afternoon, showered, napped (I presumed) in his room, then set out again toward dinnertime. For these evening forays he wore a well-brushed black topper; a black coat with silk lapels; a ruffled white shirt with a high winged collar; tight trousers, sometimes with a shiny ribbon braid stitched on the outside seam; and again, black pointed shoes. He never returned before midnight, often around two or three in the morning, sometimes never at all. In this latter case he would show up late the next morning, looking slightly worn, then disappear into his room and stay there the rest of the day, re-emerging as dapper as ever toward evening. Night was his home, his element.

"He sure does come and go," observed Stewart at our breakfast table.

"That's no concern of ours," said Mother. "He's quiet, always polite, and always prompt with the rent."

To be so close to Mr. Smythe, with only a wall between us, and yet so distant, troubled me. I treasured the slightest greeting in the hall, and the moment he returned to his room from the shower, I took a towel and hurried to the bathroom to immerse myself in the lingering steam, which still bore hints, I thought, of his scented hair and flesh. Often he left behind a sliver of fragrant green soap, expensive, probably imported; in the shower stall I lathered myself voluptuously with it, knowing that it had touched intimately that slim young body I had seen only sheathed in the most elegant clothes.

I longed to stretch out our brief encounters and sought, but never found, a pretext to knock on his door. What was his room like? I wondered. Finally I asked our maid.

"Margaret, has Mr. Smythe fixed up his room real fancy?"

"How should I know, Master Thomas? I niver been in there; it's locked. He sees to it hisself."

Now I was really curious.

One day Neil Smythe informed Mother that he would be away for a week and left no forwarding address. A carriage with a liveried coachman called for him and whisked him and his valise away to what distant revelries I could scarcely imagine. The moment he was gone, being as eager as ever to glimpse inside his room, I tried the door stealthily, but of course it was locked. So I could only pine away.

THIS WAS MY THIRD attraction. The first had begun at age twelve when, just before bed, I started playing games with myself in the mirror. Ornately framed in wood, the mirror was like the surface of a pond, a gateway to an enchanted world. Naked, I would look into it at the pale, skinny boy that I saw there, smile at him, wave to him, then duck to one side to make him disappear. Next, peeping coyly, I would make his face reappear, then his shoulders and scrawny chest, then all of him, and begin the game again. It was quite innocent; I had no special interest in my tiny little finger of a penis. But I was fascinated by this apparition, this other Tom Vaughan that appeared to me each night; he was my first lover.

My second attraction occurred in church, which I attended every Sunday with Mother, who insisted on it all the more after Stewart announced that he was done with church, it bored him, and refused to be moved by Mother's pleas and tears. She and I attended the Church of Christ and All Angels, a white marble edifice on the Avenue with red-cushioned pews and a pink marble altar. There the rector, the Reverend

Timothy Blythe, D.D., donning bright silken vestments of green or purple or white, delivered from the mahogany pulpit sermons that, being void of fire and brimstone, and any spiritual depth, rolled deliciously over you like a fountain's scented spray.

But it wasn't the elegant Reverend Blythe who attracted me – my dealings with him are another story – but, when I was fourteen, the face of a choir boy with blond hair and a delicately flushed complexion that seemed to radiate innocence and grace. I didn't know a thing about him, not even his name, but those angelic features and the warmth of his voice, which I thought I could distinguish from the others, haunted me. I asked nothing of him, only to worship the vision of his beauty; viewing it, I felt cleansed and redeemed. When, in time, that face disappeared from the ranks of the choir, never to return, I experienced an unspeakable loss. Was he, I now wonder, an image of myself?

After that, in church rarely and discreetly, and on the street more often and obviously, I began getting looks from men. It puzzled, disturbed, excited me. I scanned the mirror repeatedly. What I saw there – thick auburn hair parted in the middle, big blue eyes, smooth skin, full lips – I liked. Also my slim build, thin waist, tapering fingers. But was I good-looking? I didn't know.

Stewart caught me once at the mirror. "Primping, are we? Making ourselves pretty? Just what I'd expect from a pouf!"

I had no idea what he meant.

STEWART AND I WERE very different, he being tall with straight dark hair and cold gray eyes, while I was shorter with curly auburn hair and blue eyes. As infants, if our mother left us alone for five minutes, she would return to find me leafing through a picture book, while he would have climbed on top of the pianoforte. His dislike of me began when I was very young, and Mother would announce from the doorway of my bedroom, "Mumsey wants her little boy with her tonight, Mumsey is feeling lonely." Hearing this, I would jump out of my own bed and go running downstairs to hers, the canopied four-poster she had once shared with my father. There I soon fell asleep, reveling in the warmth of her body, the soft feel of her nightgown, the perfume of her breath. This went on for a long time – too long. Excluded from these intimacies, Stewart was jealous. Seeing me in the hall, he would scowl with rage and scorn.

"Nancy boy!"

Then too, I hadn't the slightest idea what he meant.

All through my childhood, when Stewart approached, I didn't know if he would kiss me or hit me, and neither did he. One day he would give me three marbles, then the next day take them back. Or he might offer tantalizing glimpses of what "real" boys thought about – how girls were put together, what a whiskey punch was, how to smoke cigars – then clam up, announcing I was too little to understand.

My favorite room was my father's ground-floor library, with its heavy oak writing table and sturdy glass-fronted walnut bookcases crammed with volumes that tempted me. Often, as soon as I had found a book and settled down with it, Stewart would burst in and grab my hair.

"One up or two down?"

"One up," I would say, wincing.

He yanked my hair.

"Two down," I would say, cringing.

He yanked my hair.

If I said nothing, he yanked my hair. This went on for years.

There was an unspoken agreement between us: if he didn't scare me or hurt me too much, I wouldn't tell our mother. He had a bad temper that I learned not to provoke, but it could flare up on its own, and I would be the worse for it. If a hard punch reduced me to howls of pain and our mother or the maid came running, they would scold him and threaten him with a bread-and-milk supper, but he would just slink off, bide his time, then bully me again. One evening when Aunt Jessie, who was visiting us, saw him box my ears, she boxed his ears in turn: "There, Stewart, *that's* how it feels!" He wailed in pain, left me alone for days. I welcomed her visits.

Just once, Stewart pushed me a bit too far. Having been shoved and punched for close to an hour, I snatched up a paperknife from my mother's rolltop desk and hurled it at him; it lodged in the woodwork three inches from his head. That was the only time I scared him. The nick is in the woodwork to this day.

What I wanted from Stewart was peace; what he wanted from me I never knew. We loved each other dearly.

SINCE I WAS CERTAIN that Neil Smythe, if I got to know him, would advance my education, I was annoyed and dismayed when he sent a note to Mother, announcing that he would be away for another week.

"He leads a soft life," said Stewart, whose job at the Subtreasury offered no such extended vacation.

"Now Stewart," said Mother, "we don't know what he's doing, and it's certainly no business of ours."

"Where did he write from?" I asked.

Mother glanced at the postmark. "Long Branch."

Long Branch! That popular, slightly racy resort on the Jersey shore, shunned by the pious but sought out by everyone else from the President and his cabinet on down – not quite as fashionable as Saratoga, but deliciously brazen and flash. Of course Neil Smythe was kicking up his heels there, diverted by billiard parlors, shooting galleries, faro dens, ventriloquists and conjurors, and nightly balls and hops. And here was I, stuck in the city, shuffling in my brother's hand-me-downs, fighting my way through Latin and mathematics, and subjected at intervals to Dr. Murdock's injunctions against the sin of self-pollution, which he assured us led to a blighted body and a ruined soul.

Dr. Murdock's pronouncements had of course long since piqued the curiosity of all the boys in his classes, myself included; as a result, we were all cheerfully indulging in the solitary vice, on our way to decay, debility, and death. My experiments in this direction were abetted by knowledge gleaned from a volume in my father's library whose sober gray binding masked an illustrated medical treatise discussing human anatomy with remarkable candor and far greater detail than the crude accounts occasionally offered by my brother. From it I had acquired the terms *"membrum virile"* and "orgasm," so appropriate under the circumstances. Accompanying these pleasures were fantasies focused at first on myself, with a vague peripheral other presence that gradually took the form of a tall, thin person with wavy long blond hair. What this meant, I wasn't sure.

Clarification of a kind came from Metcalf, a boy at school with a piercing glance, and broad, square shoulders and a sinewy trunk set upon well-knit hips and thighs. I found him looking at me more than once, and one day he walked me home and all but invited himself up to my room. The moment the door was shut, he grabbed me and kissed me, then announced, "Vaughan, you're a beautiful boy," at which I reddened and looked at the floor. In no time we were lying on the bed naked, sprouting prodigious erections. Since neither of us knew what to do next, we simply jerked off side by side. In the course of it I concluded that this animal lying next to me wasn't quite my cup of tea. Afterward he left quickly, and that, I thought, was that. Was I still a virgin? Regretfully I concluded that I was.

A few days later, while I was languishing in the absence of our roomer, Metcalf sought me out again after classes.

"Vaughan, tomorrow night I'm going to the Garden. Want to come along?"

"What's the Garden?"

"A beer garden on Fourth Avenue below Fourteenth Street. It's a very special place. You'll like it."

"I can't go out at night."

"Sneak out."

"I don't have a key. I couldn't get back in."

"Borrow the maid's key and copy it. That's what I did. This place is exciting. I think you'll make a hit."

Now I had to go. Tomorrow was a Friday, so there'd be no school the following day. "All right. I'll see what I can do."

Late that afternoon I managed to catch Margaret alone in the hall. A good thing, stout and loyal, she'd been with us for years. "Margaret, I have a favor to ask."

"What might that be, Master Thomas?"

"I want to borrow your key to the basement door."

"Why?"

"Never mind."

"Sure, now, you be wantin' to make a copy, don't you?"

"What if I do?"

"No, Master Thomas. It would get me in a heap of trouble."

"Mother needn't know."

"I can't risk it, Master Thomas. No!"

"Margaret, when you do the household shopping, you skim off a little of the money for yourself. Not a lot, just a little. Mother hasn't noticed."

She looked at me in fear. "I niver done it, Master Thomas, niver! Why, that would be stealin'!"

"If you give me the key, I won't say a word."

"Oh please, Master Thomas, don't be gettin' me in trouble!"

"Margaret, give me the key."

She fished in an apron pocket, handed it over. I rushed to the nearest locksmith, had it copied, came back and tried the new key in the door, then gave the old one back to Margaret. She looked anxious; I put my finger to my lips and smiled.

The next day at school I told Metcalf I would meet him at Fourth Avenue and Fourteenth Street, southwest corner, at eight.

"Make it nine. By then the place will be jumping."

"How should I dress?"

"Informal, with an open collar."

"What's this place like, anyway?"

He smiled. "Like nothing you've ever seen."

2

At 8:30 that night, fancied up in my best trousers, an open shirt, and a jacket, I tiptoed down the servants' stairs in back, inserted the big iron key in the lock, turned it gently, quietly opened the door and shut it, then locked it behind me. Striding down the street, I jingled the key with the coins in my pocket, felt free.

Metcalf was waiting at the corner in narrow striped trousers, a jacket, and a cap. He led me down Fourth Avenue to a plain brick building with shuttered windows and an imposing entrance with chipped paint, topped by LUSTGARTEN in faded lettering, leading to a dimly lit vestibule and a thick door with a peephole. Metcalf knocked, an eye scanned us through the peephole, the door opened, and a man built like a boxer waved us in.

Entering, I found myself in a large room bright with gaslight, jammed with boisterous patrons standing three-deep at a bar, chatting, singing, joking, lifting frothy mugs of beer amid tobacco fumes and wafts of smelly cheese. There were frock-coated gentlemen in toppers, boys in tight pants, workmen in jeans, and young rouged faces in gaudy dresses who didn't quite seem feminine. On the counter I glimpsed a bust of Goethe with a necklace and tiara, another of Venus topped by a derby. A few of the crowd eyed us as we stood there.

"Let's go to the garden," said Metcalf. "It's quieter there."

He led me into a large outdoor space in back with long oak tables and benches among pine trees in tubs, the whole area enclosed by latticework twined with grape vines and open to the sky above and its twinkling stars and soft full moon. It was a mild June night; kerosene lamps flickered on the tables. We found an empty table and sat. I stared around me in wonder. Men and boys, no women; aproned waiters scurrying about carrying four mugs of beer in each fist; laughter, murmurs, shouts.

"What'll it be, honeys?" A waiter had popped up out of nowhere. "Why Dick, honey, it's you!" (I'd almost forgotten that Metcalf had a first name, Dick.) "And who's your friend? Ooh, isn't he a cutie!" His weathered features beamed.

"Stevie, this is Tom. A pal of mine from school."

A quick handshake. "Welcome to the Lust Garden, as we delight to call it! I haven't seen you here before, have I?"

"My first time."

"Ooh, lucky us! So what are you boys drinking?"

I hadn't a clue, but Metcalf said, "Lager." Stevie was back in no time with two mugs of blond beer crowned with foam, and a basket of pretzels.

"There you are, sweets, it's all on the house. Cutie here" -- he indicated me – "has caused quite a stir. A new face, you know. Everybody wants to meet him, but they're shy of making a move in front of all their buddies. Imagine – *this* crowd, *shy!*"

He laughed a high-pitched laugh that sharpened the lines in his face, hurried off.

"We're getting it free?" I asked, incredulous.

"Because of you. If you show up regularly, they know you'll bring them business."

Metcalf blew off the foam on his mug, so I did the same; the froth tickled my nose. Sipping the first beer of my life, I winced: bitter. I munched some pretzels to smother the taste.

"Quite a place, isn't it?" said Metcalf.

"I've never seen anything like it. Is it always this jammed and noisy?"

"By nine o'clock, always. It's hot – the hottest place in town. For a certain crowd, that is. There are rooms upstairs you can rent. They go fast on weekends." He winked. "There's a band, too. There'll be dancing."

"Dancing? You mean men with men?"

A year before, I'd been to dancing school and made a big hit with the girls. But men dancing with men – this I had never conceived of.

"Men with men, men with boys, boys with boys. But if someone asks, you don't have to."

For a virgin, Metcalf knew a lot.

A crowd at the next table erupted in boisterous laughter.

"Never sell the Navy short," came a piping voice. "My dears, he was fabulous. Believe me, he came *buckets*!"

Another burst of laughter. Metcalf grinned; I found it offensive.

Suddenly from a small band in back came rousing strains of music. In no time the dance floor was crowded with male couples bouncing about amid yippees and yelps in some kind of polka or quadrille. Someone beckoned to Metcalf, who without a word to me scurried off; soon he was leaping and bobbing on the floor with a mustached older man in bright checked trousers. Obviously, he'd done this before.

A good-looking young man in a coat and tie, with brown hair and demure, soft eyes, sat down beside me. "May I join you? I'm Danny. What's your name?"

His smile won me over. "Tom."

"First time here?"

"Yes."

"I thought so. Want to dance?"

"Not now, not yet. I've never done it. With a man, I mean."

"Like me three years ago; you'll learn. You're a bit shy; that's nice. A fresh face, not jaded."

I looked down, at a loss for what to say.

"Tom, I'd like to introduce you to a friend. He's interesting. Can I bring him over?"

"I guess so. Sure." What else could I say?

Danny sprang up, slender and lithe, and pranced off toward the bar. The bouncy music had stopped. The band was playing "I Dream of Jeanie with the Light Brown Hair," and a young man in lederhosen and a cap with a feather was rendering it in a rich tenor voice, substituting "Johnny" for "Jeanie." Metcalf was still dancing, his arms around the older man's neck, the man's arms around his waist. The whole dance floor was now filled with couples tightly clasped and swaying gently.

Danny returned with a man of about forty in a gray tweed coat with silk-faced black lapels, who sported a fiercely waxed dark mustache and imperial that made him look a little like the emperor of France. He wore a monocle.

"Tom," said Danny, "this is my friend the Count."

I stood up and nodded. The Count shook my hand, and all three of us sat.

"Ha, ha, Count," said the man. "Slight exaggeration, but no matter. And you, lovely boy, are Tom. No last names here, of course. At bar just now I hear all around me, 'Who is that boy?...Who is that boy?...' I look, I see, I know I must say hello. I send Danny to break ice. He is my guide, my guard. Also my kept boy, very nice. Not jealous, he understands. You must understand, too. I come to make acquaintance, not seduce."

He had a smooth voice with a slight accent that didn't sound French, just vaguely European. His speech was odd but amusing; his monocle glittered in the lamplight; somehow I felt safe. He looked at me intently.

"Tommy – I call you 'Tommy,' you do not mind? – You are beautiful boy. Thick red-brown hair –"

"Auburn."

He smiled. "Yes, yes, auburn. Thick auburn hair, fine penciled eyebrows (not penciled, of course, very natural), big blue eyes, charming, pert nose, sensual lips... Yes, full, sensual lips. Wonderful. In Paris we say *petit Jésus*, little Jesus. No sacrilege intended: pretty boy. But in Paris they are commercial – little whores. You are not. You could be kept boy, something special. You are fresh, unspoiled. New to all this, no?"

"Yes."

"Charming! What age, if I may ask?"

"Sixteen."

"First bloom of youth; delightful. Perhaps you are – forgive indiscretion – virgin?"

"Yes and no."

He burst into a musical laugh. "'Yes and no' – what an answer! Can such things be in doubt? But yes, they can be. Maybe you have experience, but not enough. No?"

"Yes."

"So you are, and are not, virgin. I have great experience, I understand. You are now on brink. But not for long – too beautiful."

Listening to the Count was like hearing one of the Reverend Blythe's sermons: you just leaned back and let the froth of words flow over you. He did all the talking.

"I am in this country – how long, Danny?"

"Three weeks, two days," said Danny.

"Not long time, but I see much, do much. I want to know this raw, new land – cowboys, mountains, buffles. But first I see this raw, new city – noisy, dynamic. Second night I come here (I know from friends), meet Danny. Just like that – what luck!"

Sheepishly, Danny grinned from ear to ear.

"Nice boy, charming; for rent, but not from streets. So I rent. Not for one night, one week; for whole trip. Soon I take him West, show him his own country. Everything, I pay. Danny does not mind, likes travel. You mind I smoke?"

"Not at all." By now his talk had charmed me; I could listen forever.

He produced a long, thin cigar that he held out for Danny, who had struck a match, to light, then inhaled, exhaled. Puffs of blue haze appeared, and a rich fragrance enveloped the whole table.

"I like this place." He gestured toward the dancers, the bar. "Lust Garden – ha, ha, joke. In German, *Lustgarten* means 'pleasure garden,' nothing more. No matter: lust, pleasure – same thing. In Paris, Berlin, Amsterdam we have bars, brothels, baths – 'three b's,' I call them – with street boys, kept boys, boys who look like girls, girls who look like boys, sturdy torsos, everything. But we do not have this. So open, so democratic. Of course, as everywhere, they pay off police. But here I see doctors, lawyers, judges – once even councilman – with butchers, carpenters, laborers, artists, sailors, who knows who? All rub elbows together. Marvelous! Eros at best: manly love of comrades. As in poems of Mr. Whitman. You know Mr. Whitman?"

"I'm afraid I don't."

"What pity! Already he is read in Europe. Only New World could bring us such voice. Perhaps I give you copy, we will see. Your friend Dick, he is not coming back?"

"Still dancing with some man."

"Perhaps this is his night. Like you, he is on brink. But he is animal;

you are not. Tommy, perhaps you like carriage ride in Central Park – splendid space, so vast, so green! Tomorrow I hire carriage and take Danny. You come, too. Is vanity. To be seen in Park with one beautiful boy: wonderful. To be seen with two: more than wonderful. Yes, I am vain. Like you, like Danny. Does no harm. So you come, no?"

I had been to the Park with my mother, but this would be hugely more fun. But what if Mother or Margaret, or worse still Stewart, saw the carriage? Of course they would ask questions.

"No, I don't think I can."

"You reject invitation? I'm hurt."

"I'd like to, but my family..."

"Ah, family! Yes, is problem. What if carriage stops down street, not in front of house?"

"I'm afraid not. The neighbors..."

"I understand. You are not free, not yet. Pity. In few years all will change." Suddenly he stared at the base of my neck. "Open collar, I like. Smart of you. Byronic look – Lord Byron set fashion. He was one of us, in spite of all those ladies, oh yes. Open collar: devil-may-care, boyish. Small patch of bare skin gives idea, beneath clothes, of limber, smooth young body. I like very much."

Danny stood up. "I think we should be going."

The Count smiled. "You see, he does not trust me – not quite. Perhaps he is right. You are too attractive. But I am loyal to Danny. I am his for whole trip, and he is mine. Charming arrangement. He will see me through."

The Count stood up, bowed. I stood up, too.

"So glad to have met you, Tommy. I catch you at very special moment. You are poised to fly, have not yet flown. Perhaps I see you again, when we return from West. By then you soar. I like to see. Good luck!"

He smiled, strode off. Danny, as he followed him, looked at me and winked. I was left at the table with a trace of blue haze and a hint of fragrant tobacco. For me, the whole conversation had been something of a dream: delightful, strange, unreal.

Metcalf returned with the mustached man in checked trousers, whom he didn't introduce. "My big night. He's got a room; we're going upstairs." With that, he was off, following his companion toward the back. So Metcalf was no longer on the brink; he was plunging.

I felt conspicuous at the table alone, and it was late. Leaving my half-finished mug of beer, I got up and headed for the front. As I passed through the noisy barroom, a rouged apparition with bright gold hair, in a skirt with jangly bells, loomed in front of me, said "Good-bye, sweets!" and kissed me on the cheek. I hurried out.

Returning home, I sneaked in quietly and tiptoed up the back stairs, avoiding steps that I remembered as creaking. Safe in my room at last, I felt relieved, excited, confused. I had a lot to think about. Tired, I dropped in bed, slept soundly.

The next day no one said anything; my absence had passed unnoticed. All that weekend I was in a dreamlike state. A train of images obsessed me: the Count's glittering monocle, Venus in a derby, rouged young faces, Goethe in a necklace, the waiter whose lined features belied his youthful exuberance, boys in tight pants, dancers pressed so close together that each couple seemed to be one. In the privacy of my room I hummed, then softly sang:

I dream of Johnny with the light brown hair
Borne, like a vapor, on the summer air...

Then, still humming, I clasped myself tightly and, eyes shut, rocked gently to the music. But in these fantasies I now imagined a companion clasping me who was tall, thin, and blond.

I couldn't hide my mood from Mother.

"My boy is wistful, isn't he?"

"Mmm."

"Maybe he's in love. He's the age."

"Mmm."

"One of the girls from dancing school, I'll bet."

"Mmm."

"Well, don't worry, I won't tell Stewart."

With that, she dropped the subject. And I had discovered the usefulness of the noncommittal murmur.

When I saw Metcalf in class on Monday, he winked at me but didn't say a word, and after school left quickly. I was disappointed, having expected a full account of his deflowering.

Beautiful boy: the words burned through my brain. Murmuring them, time and again I looked in the mirror, saw nothing I hadn't seen before. But on the street I garnered glances – some bold and inviting, some guarded – and was soon savoring the prodigious pleasure of being looked at with desire.

3

LATE ONE AFTERNOON, SOON after I'd returned from school, I saw another open carriage with a liveried coachman stop in front of our house and deposit Neil Smythe and his valise on the pavement. Immediately I rushed down the stoop to help him with his luggage, for which he graced me with a smile. I took it all the way up to his room, and it was just as well, for Mr. Smythe looked rather worn out. There was no conversation whatsoever. After a quick thanks, he shut the door and locked it, and wasn't seen again that day. Tired from partying, he was probably catching up on his sleep.

That same afternoon Mother received a letter from Aunt Jessie, announcing her arrival the very next day. Aunt Jessie lived in Boston and twice a year visited one married daughter in Albany and another in Philadelphia; when visiting the one in Philadelphia, she stopped off to see us on the way. Mother had to renounce a long-planned foray to the Hospital for the Ruptured and Crippled, where the Dames of Charity, a formidable band of Samaritans from the Reverend Blythe's church, would hand out tracts and cookies. We were all a bit nervous.

Late the following afternoon, when her cab pulled up in front of the house, Stewart and I ran out to collect a brief greeting and kiss, then followed with her luggage as she marched up the stoop. A powerfully whaleboned widow of middle years with an aggressive nose and bright, even teeth, she consigned her bonnet and parasol to Margaret in the hallway, then entered the parlor to greet my mother with a vigorous embrace. She described her trip from Boston by train and steamboat as wearisome; squinted through a lorgnette at a marble greyhound and pronounced it abominable; labeled as "morbid" a stuffed bird under a bell jar on a whatnot; and chuckled, as she always did, at an upward soaring Venus in oils – an apotheosis, so Mother had informed us -- attended by cupids with masked genitals. Only after she had done her best to demolish Mother's pretensions to the House Beautiful, did she give serious attention to her hosts.

"How have you been, my dear Susanna? In the pink of health, no doubt. As for me, don't ask, I'm wretched."

"You look blooming," Mother insisted.

"Like a pinched bouquet. Which the noxious fumes of this city, with its stinking stables, uncollected garbage, and gas works will further deteriorate. I shan't stay long." (A proud Bostonian, she had a low opinion of New York.) "Stewart, Thomas, come let me look at you!"

A familiar ritual: she examined us through her jewel-handled lorgnette.

"Stewart, you have attained your manly luster. You've given up spitting, I hope. Spit is an excrement of the body, to be disposed of privately, with care."

"Yes, Aunt Jessie," said Stewart.

"Good manners separate well-conducted people from the mechanic and laboring classes. I get a whiff of bad company off of you, ardent spirits and the flagrant weed – cigars, no doubt. Not surprising at your age, but we shall keep it in check. You've stopped bullying your brother,

I hope?"

"We get along…sort of."

"Hmm. You should have put that behind you by now. What kind of employment do you have?"

"I have a position with the Subtreasury." Stewart had long since completed his dubious career at Dr. Murdock's academy.

"Oh? What kind of a position?"

"Well…clerk."

"Subassistant subclerk is more like it," I put in.

Stewart shot me a look of rage.

"That will do, Thomas," said Aunt Jessie. "I'll get to you in a minute. Stewart, I assume that you help your mother meet the household expenses."

"I do what I can."

"Which, I assume, means not very much. You need a better job."

Stewart stared awkwardly at the floor. Next, she turned to me.

"Thomas, is that down on your chin, or fuzz from the upholstery?"

"Down," I said emphatically.

"So you too are approaching man's estate. What age are you, and how far along in school?"

"Sixteen. I'm in my junior year, Aunt Jessie."

"One more to go. These are your formative years. Please look at me when I speak to you."

"Yes, Aunt Jessie." I had been eyeing her heavy brooch of turquoise set with pearls. Her jewelry always fascinated me. It was hard and glittery; she wore it with style and flair.

"And what are your favorite classes?"

"English and Latin."

"Excellent. You will recite for me later. By all means read the poets, however deplorable their morals. You will learn more from them than from the twaddle dispensed by your teachers."

"Yes, Aunt Jessie."

"You still go to church?"

"Every Sunday, with Mother." It was hardly a chore; several mustachioed parishioners had been eyeing me.

"Hopefully it won't do too much harm. Some of the hymns are acceptable. In time, you'll sort it all out for yourself."

Aunt Jessie, as Mother never tired of warning us, was an incorrigible freethinker.

Suddenly she gave me a searching look. "Thomas, for a sixteen-year-old you're seemingly much too well behaved. I wonder what you're up to..."

The woman was uncanny. I looked at her with big innocent eyes, said nothing.

"And now, both of you come kiss your aunt."

We did, dutifully. I never minded the gesture, reveling in the whiffs of perfume and smell of clean satin and lace that emanated from her person, not to mention, sometimes, the touch of gold and jet.

After dinner that evening we all assembled in the upstairs sitting room, where my aunt settled herself in a blue velvet armchair. There I recited Keats's "Ode to a Nightingale" to her satisfaction and Stewart's visible annoyance. Then she fixed him with a look.

"Stewart, have you been keeping your mother's books, as I instructed you?"

"Yes, Aunt Jessie."

"Good. Bring them here!"

From a rolltop desk in the corner he produced a stack of account books. When I had last seen them, in the time of Mother's governance, they had been covered with dust and crammed with little pieces of paper – Mother's haphazard jottings – which, when the books were opened, had swirled and fluttered to the floor. Now, the books looked clean and neat. As Jessie inspected them, giving special attention to the current one, we all watched nervously.

"Legible and reasonably coherent," she pronounced, handing them back to my brother. "And you sold the carriage?"

"Oh yes," said Mother. "A great sacrifice, but we did it."

For Mother the carriage, like the unused pianoforte in the parlor, was a symbol of affluence.

"And we've taken in a lodger," I volunteered.

"Yes indeed," said Mother. "A very elegant young gentleman of means. He just returned from Long Branch yesterday."

"Did he?" said Aunt Jessie. "Hmm. It's rather early in the season for Long Branch, nor do I recommend the place: too risqué. I much prefer Saratoga."

"He's quite genteel," Mother insisted.

"I'll be the judge of that. See to it that I meet him before I depart this odorous city tomorrow morning."

Neil Smythe and Aunt Jessie face to face: an encounter that might prove interesting. I looked forward to it.

At breakfast the following morning Aunt Jessie issued another pronouncement: "Stewart must get a better job. Clerking at the Subtreasury is hardly appropriate."

"Good jobs are hard to get," protested Stewart. "You need connections."

"And you shall have them. I'll give you a letter of introduction to a partner in your late father's Wall Street firm, with whom I still do business. They'll hire you or I'll know why. Aside from the advance in salary, a clerkship there can have interesting possibilities."

Aunt Jessie wasn't one to shilly-shally. When Stewart left for work after breakfast, he had the promised letter in his possession.

"Now where is this lodger of yours?" she then demanded.

"I think he's sleeping late," I explained.

"Hmm." (Jessie's *hmm*s were resonant with censure.) "Well then, I shall look at him next time."

When she left an hour later, Mother and I saw her out to her cab, piled her luggage in, and said good-bye. She was wearing a seven-inch butterfly clasp at her waist that fascinated me, and a bonnet adorned with loops of velvet and — the latest fashion — a bird's nest with eggs (it amused me to think they might hatch). Whatever she wore, whether chic, startling, or preposterous, she always brought it off.

When Jessie kissed Mother good-bye, she enjoined her, "See that Stewart uses that letter to get a good job. Soon enough we'll be getting him married, which won't be easy, since in this city there are more prostitutes than marriageable virgins!"

With that, she was off, an unsettling mix of fairy godmother and angel of doom.

AFTER A FEW DAYS Neil Smythe resumed his pattern of going out for a late morning breakfast, then returning by late afternoon and setting out again toward dinnertime, always dressed in the height of fashion. We exchanged brief greetings in the hallway, but he seemed as elusive as ever. Then one afternoon there came a knock on my door, and I opened to find myself face to face with his fine-boned features, his eyes like green jewels.

"Tom, I've been thinning out my wardrobe. Could you use this cravat? I'm tired of it." He held out a yellow silk cravat.

"Yes, I could, Mr. Smythe," I stammered. "Thank you." I took it, meeting his gaze for an instant before looking down at the floor.

"It goes well with a green shirt or a blue one. And why don't you call me Neil?"

With that, he was gone. This abominable habit of mine of casting my eyes at the floor! Shutting the door, I looked at the cravat, touched it, caressed it: soft, sensual. Alas, I had no green or blue shirt to go with it, only dull, conventional white! My whole wardrobe seemed deficient: no pants with a thin stripe of braid down the side, no tasseled walking stick; shoes that were square-toed, blunt. Nothing suitable for a dapper sortie into those mild summer nights where Neil Smythe was vanishing mysteriously. My life was drab indeed.

School ended. I wouldn't see Metcalf or the other boys till fall; most of them were traveling with their families. Then, late one morning, my curiosity got the better of me: when Neil Smythe left the house, I followed him at what I thought was a discreet distance. He strode briskly toward the Avenue, his walking stick tapping the pavement rhythmically in a show of self-assurance and pride. Where was he going? Now at last I would find out.

When he reached the Avenue, he stopped, turned, and looked directly at me. Caught, I froze on the spot and blushed to the quick. He then smiled, resumed his stride, turned the corner, and disappeared.

Rushing home, I brooded in my room. Of course he had seen me and knew what I was up to! His smile had shown not a trace of anger, but I was chagrinned and felt a deep sense of guilt; I simply couldn't face him. That day and the next I managed to avoid him. Then, on the third day, Mother informed me that he was leaving town for a month and had given her forwarding addresses not just for Long Branch but for Newport and Saratoga as well: he was hitting all the resorts! This news brought me relief and frustration. The next morning I watched discreetly from a front window, as he once again got into a sleek black carriage and was whisked away.

What delights awaited him at those resorts? Would he be dancing rowdy quadrilles with men like I had seen at the Garden, then pairing off with them for voluptuous secret pleasures? More likely, he would be cavorting with women – worldly women who read French novels, traveled, frequented shooting galleries, waltzed rapturously, and didn't go to church. Whatever he was up to, it was vastly more interesting than my life of desolation, spiced at intervals with moony fantasies where, eyes shut, I hugged myself and swayed dreamily, while crooning "Johnny with the Light Brown Hair."

Meanwhile Aunt Jessie's letter had worked marvels: Stewart was hired as a clerk in the brokerage house and was soon dazzling us with talk of pools and margin, bulls and bears, puts and calls and straddles. This, and his rigorous keeping of the household accounts, let him play lord of the manor.

"Creampuff can loll around now," he announced, "but when he finishes school, he's going to get a job, too."

"Stewart," said Mother, "don't call your brother names."

"Little Darling," vowed Stewart, "is going to pull his weight in the world!"

IN AUGUST MOTHER'S TWO benevolent societies, the Dames of Charity and the Society for the Relief of Aged Indigent Females, suspended good works for a month, while the ladies took themselves off to resorts or country villas with their families. We, of course, were trapped in the city by our budget. While neighbors were noisily packing luggage into express wagons and stepping gaily into carriages, Mother pulled the front blinds down and never ventured out on the street. This subterfuge, I was sure, fooled no one; I was glad it wasn't witnessed by our roomer.

As the worst summer heat settled in, I moped about the house sipping iced syrups and wielding a fan, then in the afternoon napped on my bed stark naked. Not even the books in my father's library held me.

Inevitably, my thoughts reverted to the Garden. Though hesitant to go there alone, I sneaked out of the house one evening, got halfway there, turned back. Another time I made it all the way to the heavy oak door at the entrance, but the thought of being scanned through the peephole unnerved me; I didn't knock. Returning home, I cursed myself; it did no good.

In September our neighbors returned from their summer vacations with a great clatter of trunks being unloaded from express wagons and carried up steep front stoops. Mother put aside *Little Women*, which she had been reading avidly, raised the front blinds, and let herself be seen again on the street. But of our roomer, not a sign.

School resumed; I was glad. When I saw Metcalf again, he looked downcast. "It's over," he told me after classes, meaning, I assumed, the affair with the mustached man he had danced with. He seemed wiser, more subdued. "Let's go to the Garden tomorrow," he suggested.

I leaped at the chance.

Once again the sneaking out at night, the meeting with Metcalf on the corner, the approach, heart thumping, to the heavy oak door with the peephole; but this time -- at last! -- I went in.

In the barroom we found again the glow of gaslight, a thick crowd, loud talk, tobacco fumes, laughter. I gave a quick glance at the drinkers, and there not twelve feet away from me, standing at the bar with an older man, was Neil Smythe. Our eyes locked; he didn't bat a lash.

"That blond one at the bar..." I whispered to Metcalf.

"You know him?"

"He rooms with us."

Metcalf whistled softly, "Kid, you keep good company. He's the most sought-after kept boy in the city."

Panic swept over me. Without a word I spun about and fled.

4

BACK IN MY ROOM at home, thoughts raced through my mind. Of course: his comings and goings, the fancy clothes, the carriages – how could I have missed it? Easily: I was new to the game. But what was such a life like? Did he have one friend or many? If they gave him money, what was he expected to do for it? Whatever his life was, certainly he seemed to be enjoying it. But was there room in it for me? Everything about him disturbed and fascinated me. Who was he, anyway, and what was he like?

In class the next day Metcalf whispered to me, "See me after class." When I did, he asked, "Why did you run off?"

"I don't know. Seeing him there, I was scared, confused. Too confused to talk to him, I guess."

"Well *he* wants to talk to *you*."

"How do you know?"

"He told me. I gabbed with him and his friend. He's returning to your place today. Go home. He'll be waiting for you."

"Why does he want to see me?"

"How should I know? Go home!"

I did. I wasn't in my room five minutes, when he knocked at the door.

"Can I come in, Tom? I think we should talk."

I waved him in. He was wearing a lounge jacket and narrow gray trousers, and those famous silk-lined black velvet slippers. We sat, he in a chair and I on the bed. This vacation seemed to have agreed with him; he didn't look worn.

"I don't know why I ran off like that," I blurted out.

"Don't worry about it. How long have you been going there?"

"Since June. But last night was only the second time."

"That's why I haven't seen you. I go there often. There's no other place quite like it, just a few dingy bars and the baths. I've wanted to talk to you right from the start, but I held off; you're so young. How old are you, anyway?"

"Almost seventeen."

"Sixteen, and you look still younger. In some ways, an advantage. You know about me, of course; Dick told you."

"He said you're the most sought-after kept boy in the city."

He smiled. "That's flattering, though I know some other boys who might be minded to argue it. Right now I'm not being kept, but yes, I sleep with men for money. I don't have to, but I like it; it's fun."

"What do you do?"

"Whatever they want, within reason. I pleasure them. And so will you, in time."

"What do you mean?"

"The young men at the Garden, to use the lingo, are either sturdies, poufs, or b.b.'s. The sturdies are the masculine ones, well muscled and robust; lots of men go for them. The poufs are the nancy boys, very effeminate: wigs or dyed hair, mincing gestures, rouge, and all that. They can grate on you, but they can also be fun."

"And the b.b.'s?"

"Beautiful boys. Not poufs, not sturdies; in between. Feminine in some ways, but not effeminate. Passive, attractive, eager to please. Boys, always boys, not men. That's you, that's me."

As he spoke, the strangest feeling came over me; I felt vulnerable, exposed. Until now we'd barely spoken, but he seemed to know me to the core. Our eyes met; his weren't green, as I had thought, but gray-green with flecks of gold around the pupil: a searching gaze, direct.

"Now I'm going to be very indiscreet. Are you a virgin, Tom?"

That question again! "More or less. People look at me, but nothing seems to happen."

"Maybe you don't want it to."

"I do!"

"You're very good-looking; that may put them off. Things usually happen when they're meant to happen."

"Maybe they're meant to happen now."

Without thinking, I'd just blurted it out. Mother and Stewart were away; Margaret was with the cook in the kitchen.

He smiled. "Are you sure?"

My heart was thumping. "Yes!"

"That's going pretty fast, don't you think?"

"I'm tired of waiting!"

"You're so young."

"How old were you when you started?"

"Hmm, your age."

"Well then!"

"All right, but I'll be gentle."

He sat beside me on the bed, ran his fingers through my hair; I liked it. Then he kissed me; I liked it even more. Then I kissed him like crazy, and he held me off a bit.

"Easy, easy; not so fast. These things have a rhythm."

He undressed me, then himself. I rushed to push a chair against the door, came back. Gently he caressed my body, sculpting each contour with his hands, till I became a mindless little animal, hugely excited, pliant to his will. Guided by him, I lay back on the bed and he pleasured me, bringing me deftly to completion. When he released me, I felt wonderfully spent, obliterated, like in a thousand pieces. Pressing up against him, I felt his arm around me in a nest of warmth and comfort that I didn't want ever to leave. Finally he sat up.

"I haven't had a boy in a long time. I'd forgotten what fun it can be. Tom, you have possibilities."

I sat up too and looked at him. "Neil, I love you."

"No you don't," he said softly.

"I do!"

"You can't, you mustn't. Remember what I do for a living. I'm attracted to older men. We can have affection, but love – real love – is out of the question."

"I love you. I've loved you for months!"

"No, you want me, or think you do, but you really want to be *like* me; there's a difference. Trust me. I know you better than you do, because I know myself. We're b.b.'s. We exist to pleasure men. We'll talk some more tomorrow. Right now we'd better get dressed, and I'll get back to my room. Your mother and brother will soon be home."

We dressed and kissed; he left. I was puzzled and confused, but at least I wasn't a virgin anymore. And his words haunted me: *We exist to pleasure men.*

AT SCHOOL THE NEXT day I was in a muddle. I felt hugely different yet somehow the same; it was strange. Inattentive to my studies, I kept thinking of Neil Smythe's supple, smooth young body and the knowing touch of his hands. That afternoon, dodging Metcalf, I hurried home and knocked on his door.

"Come in, Tom."

I went in and stared all around. What had been a rather bare room with minimal furniture had been transformed. There were vases of flowers, a potted fern, and a bureau top backed by a big gilt mirror, with a rich glinty clutter of things, a smaller mirror tilting in a frame, and a daguerreotype of himself looking splendidly distant and poised. A silk tie lay over the back of an armchair; beside the wardrobe was a neat double rank of boots and shoes, all polished. Everywhere, whether from soap or cologne or one of those little aromatic bags like the ones my mother suspended in her wardrobe, a subtle fragrance permeated all. It was magic.

"You like the place – how I've fixed it up?" He was wearing his lounge jacket and the black velvet slippers.

"Yes! It's marvelous! Can I see your things?"

"Of course."

He opened the wardrobe, showed me trousers for afternoon calls and evening wear, white and colored shirts, cravats of every hue, top hats and derbies on pegs. In a drawer of his bureau were pearl-gray and lavender and cream kid gloves, and in a glass dish on top of it, jeweled cufflinks, a diamond tiepin, rings. He let me finger the ivory-headed walking stick that tapped on the pavement so rhythmically, and touch a gold-headed cane.

"I wish I had stuff like this!"

"You can, if you want to, in time."

"By pleasuring men?"

"Of course. But only when you're ready."

"I'm ready now!"

"That remains to be seen. Where are you in school?"

"Just one year to go. But now it seems pretty irrelevant."

"It isn't. Manners and education count. That's what will make you different from the street boys. There are street boys all over the place selling themselves; they're coarse, and some men like that. But a beautiful boy who's well bred and schooled – that's special. There aren't many of them; they're in demand. That's how I get on."

"Then I want to be like you."

"Finish school first."

"School's a bore!"

"You really think you'd like this life?"

"Yes! I'm tired of being Mama's little boy. I'm tired of Stewart calling me a sweet little stay-at-home goody-goody, while he's out having adventures."

"Doesn't his job keep him busy?"

"Not so busy he can't go out on the town with his friends. Meanwhile I'm stuck at home in his hand-me-downs."

"Hmm, I see."

"I want to go out like you do, and have the nice things you have. And I like being looked at by men. I like it a lot."

"All right, but there's more to it than that. You've still got a lot to learn."

"Like what?"

"To satisfy a man, you can't just lie back and let him do all the work. You've got to do something, too. That's what he's paying you for. You need a whole bag of tricks."

"Then show me. I'll learn."

"You want lessons?"

"Yes! Teach me everything you know."

"Hmm. I hadn't quite thought of that: formal lessons in providing pleasure."

"Why not?"

"Some people would say it's crazy. I'd be fostering the competition."

"I couldn't compete with you."

"That's what you think. If I launched you, you might go far. But as for lessons, how could we manage it?"

"Stewart works, and in the afternoons Mother's out a lot with the Aged Indigents and the Dames. If I come straight home from school, we'd have close to two hours before either of them gets home. In the afternoon Margaret stays downstairs."

"Seems risky, even so. Doesn't your mother have her lady friends over?"

"Oh yes, her sister toilers in the vineyard. But those days would be the best of all, since she's busy then gabbing with her guests, and Margaret's serving them goodies. They'd never notice a thing."

"You're persuasive, and it might be fun. I'll do it on two conditions. First, you have to do everything I tell you."

"I will!"

"Second, you have to finish school. I'll even come to your graduation. Agreed?"

"School? Oh, all right."

"So when shall we start?"

"Now!"

So began my higher education.

5

WE TOOK OUR CLOTHES off and lay on the bed; it had scented sheets. In no time he had me excited. Sitting on the bed's edge, he pressed me down to my knees. It was obvious what he wanted, so I did it; he ran his fingers through my hair. It happened very fast. Afterward we lay back on the bed in silence. I felt strange. Slowly we came out of it.

"Tom, that was great. Are you all right? How do you feel?"

"Funny. Squeamish, I guess, just a little."

"So did I at first. You'll get used to it and then you'll love it."

"Don't other people find it...well...disgusting?"

"Of course. So what? Go by your own experience. You and I are cocksuckers and we're good at it, and you'll get better still. It's the most beautiful act of love I know."

Cocksuckers...Never before had I heard that word used so casually, and in praise. It had always been spoken in anger, scorn, or disgust. By word and deed, Neil Smythe was taking me places where I'd never been and never thought to be. I went back to my room in a daze. "Cocksucking is beautiful," I whispered to myself in bed every night that week, then on the street and even in church. It thrilled me. This was an adventure.

I WASN'T MOONY ANYMORE. The days when Tommy Vaughan hugged himself and, eyes shut, swayed to the languorous strains of "Jeanie" were gone forever; I couldn't believe I'd ever been so stupid. I was preoccupied all right, but with luscious thoughts of lust. Mother still thought me smitten.

"Head over heels, is it?"

"Mmm."

"No hope?"

"Mmm."

"Poor Tom. Well, it will pass."

"NOW WE'LL DO IT the other way," Neil announced at our next session, grinned, and pinched my behind.

"I'm not keen on the back-door stuff."

"Me neither, but it's a part of the repertoire. There are always those who want it."

He yanked off my clothes and spanked me. Instantly I became again the mindless little animal that he could do with as he pleased. Then, having put me naked on the bed, face down, and greased me with some slick kind of jelly, he very gently entered me, probing deeper and deeper. It was overwhelming. He spent, then withdrew. There was a sensation deep inside me, not quite pain, that I didn't like.

"God, I feel raped." My eyes were tearing.

"Not raped, just totally had. For a beginner you did pretty good."

I was crying now; he stroked me.

"You'll be all right, Tom. There, there, you'll be all right."

I buried my face in his chest and wept.

IN NOVEMBER AUNT JESSIE invaded us again wearing a hat with stuffed birds, clinking jewelry, and a fur-trimmed shawl; something always had to die so she could wear it. At her command, Stewart brought the account books; she looked at them again and approved.

"Stewart, you have a new look of responsibility. How is that job going?"

"Fine, Aunt Jessie. I just got a raise. I'm mastering the intricacies of bonds. Western railroads are very interesting. The continent will soon be spanned."

"Interesting, you say? We'll talk about it later. I trust you feel as secure on the inside as you appear to be on the outside."

To this, Stewart said nothing.

"Thomas, come over here so I can look into those big blue eyes. Hmm...You have a knowing look you never had before. I wonder why."

"In school we're reading Virgil and Milton. They're expanding my experience of the world." (I didn't mention Catullus, whom I'd discovered in my father's library, and who when not banging his ladylove Lesbia, was screwing slave boys.)

"With all due respect to the poets, I don't think that explains it. You're hiding something. You're hiding a lot."

Once again I looked at her with all the innocence that I could muster, but this time it wasn't very much.

During her visit she finally met Neil briefly; I wasn't there.

"Quite the fancy Dan, isn't he?" she opined to us afterward. "Stylish clothes, expensive. I wonder where the money comes from."

"He's a gentleman of independent means," said Mother. "And so genteel."

"Hmm. Well, those manners are appreciated, but it's all a bit calculated; no spontaneity. He smiles, but he doesn't laugh."

True enough, I'd never seen Neil laugh.

The next day, after further comments on the city's foul smells in-
doors and out, and on my knowing look, she departed, leaving me more
unsettled than usual.

"TODAY WE'LL TRY BONDAGE," said Neil. "I think you're ready for it."

Once again we were in his locked room, standing naked face to face.

"Turn around and put your wrists together behind you."

I did. He tied them with a stretch of rope. When I faced him again,
there was a hard look in his eye.

"Now you're my prisoner. I can do with you what I please."

Already I was nervous; I didn't like this game.

"You've committed shameful offenses; you will be punished."

What offenses? What was he talking about?

"Get down on your knees."

For once, I didn't want to.

"Get down on your knees!

He had almost shouted; I sank to my knees.

"Slave, you will do anything I tell you to do, no matter how vile or
disgusting."

I nodded.

"Repeat that. And look me in the eye when you do."

I repeated it, staring into his cold gray-green eyes. A strange passiv-
ity had crept over me; I seemed to have no will of my own.

"Do me."

I did, feverishly; anything to get this over with. We were finished in
no time; he lay back on the bed. I was still kneeling, head down, sunk
in depths of shame.

"Hey, you were pretty good."

Dazed, I looked up; he was smiling. This seemed to be the Neil I
knew. Confused, I didn't budge.

"Get up, Tom, get up!"

Slowly I got up and joined him on the bed.

"It's just a game; I don't do whips and chains." He nudged me. "Hey, it's okay; you'll get used to it."

I nodded, half convinced, and after a few minutes went to my room in a stupor.

In my dreams that night I was in a double column of young men in prison clothes, all handcuffed to a long chain between the two columns, our feet shackled, attended by sneering guards, like pictures I had seen in *Harper's Weekly*. Though ordered to march, we could only shuffle, taking very short steps. "Bad boys!" bellowed one of the guards. "Bad boys are going before Judgy. Judgy will punish bad boys!" A host of bystanders were watching; we stared at the ground in shame. What our crimes were, who Judgy was, and what punishments awaited us, never became clear. I woke up, my face burning, my penis brazenly erect. I had discovered, on some deep, unfathomable level, the mysterious link between pleasure and shame.

A week passed before our next session; Neil had other commitments. When I saw him again, he announced, "Now we'll turn it around." This time he had me tie his wrists behind him, and told me to play the master. I tried, couldn't; my heart wasn't in it. "I guess I flunk this class."

"We'll see. When you look at me, think of someone who's abused you, someone you hate. Someone you'd give anything to get even with, someone you'd like to dominate."

Suddenly I didn't see Neil, but my brother. He was smirking, with the surly thrust lip of the bully. Years of resentment surfaced; I seethed.

"You shit, you vile stinking turd. You brainless thug, swagger and fists can't save you, under that flimsy mask you haven't an ounce of manhood, your tool is limp, you're less than a nance, a pouf! Get down on your knees, scum, for punishment."

Surprised, he did, showing puzzlement, then a hint of fear.

I towered over him. "Pig, eat my slime!"

He did. When I shot, he wrenched away from me and retched on the floor. I was stunned. It wasn't Stewart anymore, it was Neil, and he was vomiting.

"Holy God, what's happening? Neil, are you all right? I'm sorry, I'm sorry, I'm sorry!"

He waved me away, still retching.

"What came over me? Oh God, Neil, I'm so sorry!" I fetched a towel, gave it to him.

Slumped over, he sat on the floor, breathing heavily, a dazed look on his face. Taking the towel, he wiped off his chin, looked at me. A faint smile.

"Things got out of hand," he said.

I helped him up, sat him on the bed. "You're all right, aren't you? Aren't you?"

He nodded. "Just give me a minute."

I wiped up the vomit with the towel, then tossed it in a corner. He lay back, held my hand.

"No more bondage," he said.

"No. No more bondage."

We had glimpsed our roily depths.

When I next passed my brother in the hall, his lips curled at once in derision and he was on the verge of a comment, but when he saw the look I gave him, he shut up, hurried off.

ON NEW YEAR'S DAY it was the custom for ladies to receive, and for gentlemen to go out calling. Helped by Cook and Margaret, Mother awaited her callers – church friends and husbands of the other lady toilers – with a generous spread of little cakes and custards and a decanter of nonalcoholic punch: a blend of fruit juices recommended by Cora Worthington's *Joyful Abstinence Cookbook*. By mutual agreement, Stewart and I would make our calls separately. Recently, on my seventeenth birthday, I had extracted a front-door key from Mother and now, during the day, could come and go freely; this was my first time making calls. The ladies I called on were the girls of the dancing class, frilled and beribboned creatures like candy in fancy wrappings, which indeed they were. I charmed their mamas, flirted and flattered, and gorged myself on plum cakes and currant buns. When one lacy little virgin, pink and giggly, popped gingersnaps into my mouth, I tried to kiss her fingers. I was a great success; several of the young ladies, I was certain, had a crush on me.

Neil too was making the rounds, as he reported to me later: besides my mother, an assortment of reigning society queens, kept women, fallen women, actresses, one house-proud brothel keeper, one flourishing abortionist – a randier crowd than mine by a long shot, and one that, in time, I hoped to glimpse. He too, I'm sure, was a hit.

I KNEW NOW THAT I didn't love Neil; he was like an older brother – the brother I should have had but didn't. I could tell him anything and not feel judged.

"Neil, those tight pants they wear at the Garden…" We were in his room, following one of my lessons.

He grinned. "Nut huggers. I have several pairs, but I don't wear them when calling on your mother."

"I want me a pair."

"I wonder why. Well, if you can scrape up the money, I'll take you to my tailor; he's the best."

"How much would they cost?"

"Material and tailoring, at least ten dollars."

I was crestfallen. "My allowance falls far short of that."

"Hmm…Tell you what, I'll stake you to them."

"Why?"

"I can afford it, and you'll look fetching. I want to see you strut."

So he took me to his tailor, Mr. Fanshaw on Sixth Avenue, a fancy shop upstairs. On the double doors in stylish lettering: FANSHAW'S THE EPITOME OF FASHION. Inside, customers were studying themselves in full-length mirrors, attended by clerks with tapes. Seeing Neil, Mr. Fanshaw came over at once: a short man of about forty, with a slick black mustache curled at the tips.

"Why, Mr. Smythe, good to see you! It's been a while. What can I do for you?"

"My young friend here wants a pair of nut huggers. Tom, this is Mr. Willard. He'll take care of you."

We shook hands; he looked at me and smiled.

"Yes, most appropriate. Quite popular in certain circles. Plain, plaid, checked, or striped?"

"Plain, I think," said Neil.

"With braid down the side," I put in.

"All right," said Neil. "With braid."

Mr. Fanshaw showed us samples in red, green, and fawn. "Red is all the rage right now. Very vibrant, quite assertive."

"I like it!" I said. "It's exciting."

"Too exciting," said Neil. "Green will do, with blue braid down the side."

I didn't argue; he knew best.

"If our young friend will just hold still, I'll take the measurements." Mr. Fanshaw produced a tape.

While he measured me from crotch to cuff, his fingers were a bit too active; I was annoyed yet rather liked it.

"Hip pockets?" Mr. Fanshaw asked.

"Absolutely not," said Neil.

"I'll need two weeks," said the tailor. "We're terribly busy right now. Come on the twentieth. Agreed?"

"Fine," said Neil.

"Our young friend will look quite smashing. A heartbreaker, for sure." He smiled, took Neil's deposit, and hurried off.

Two weeks later we returned. I tried on the pants; Neil approved and paid, Fanshaw beamed. "Yes," he said, "smashing!"

In my room that night I postured in front of the mirror. My bottom was nicely contoured; in front there was a hint of a bulge. I couldn't wait to be seen at the Garden.

I DIDN'T WEAR THEM to my graduation in June. Attending the ceremony were Mother and Aunt Jessie; Stewart, coerced by Mother; and Neil, whose presence delighted Mother, surprised as she was that her elegant roomer took such an interest in her son's education. Which was true enough: for the preceding month he had suspended our sessions, so I could concentrate on my studies, as a result of which I passed my exams with top honors and became class valedictorian, giving the farewell address at commencement.

My theme was the Socratic injunction: know thyself. To cope with life's trials and toils, I declaimed, we must shed illusions, shun the squeamish prejudices of the hoi polloi (though ignorant of it, I loved to throw in scraps of Greek), escape false self-perceptions, kneel to the Good, the True, and the Beautiful, and above all, through thick and thin, trust to our own experience. While I spoke, Dr. Murdock nodded his whiskered features in assent, Stewart fidgeted, Mother and Aunt Jessie beamed, and Neil nursed a faint, sly smile. Then the chaplain prayed, Dr. Murdock orated endlessly on our going forth into the highways of commerce or the groves of academe, and the diplomas were distributed. A hubbub of farewells followed; Metcalf winked at me: "See you around, kid. You know where."

Mother served a fancy dinner for all of us, Neil included, in my honor, and Aunt Jessie gave me a handsome gold watch, but my real reward came two nights later, when Neil took me to the Garden. I wore my nut huggers with my schoolboy's cap and waist-length jacket, affording to all a rich glimpse of my bottom. When we danced, I got plenty of attention.

"This is nothing," said Neil. "Tomorrow the real fun begins. I've got plans for you."

"What?"

"You'll see."

6

"HERE'S THE DEAL," NEIL told me in his room the next day. "I've taught you the basics. What you need now is experience. You're supposed to get a job, aren't you?"

"My brother says he'll kill me if I don't."

"All right, you're going to go to work for Young America, a new messenger service on Broadway run by a Mr. Neddy. Only you won't be delivering messages; you'll be delivering yourself."

"Huh?"

"The messenger service is just a façade, a front. Young America provides well-bred, beautiful boys to older gentlemen of means."

"It's a brothel?"

"Not really. The office is just an office; the boys go to the clients' lodgings. Very discreet. Likewise very selective. No street boys; well-mannered young men like you and me. And the clients are screened; no weirdies, no rough stuff unless completely agreed to. To be serviced, the clients have to be known to the management. Which is a great protection for the boys. I know; I've been working there for two months."

"You're getting connected through them?"

"Constantly. With doctors, lawyers, merchants, a commissioner or two: an impressive clientele."

"And they pay?"

"Through the nose. Young America takes a hefty slice of my earnings, but their fee is so high, I'm still better off with them than on my own. And it's safer and more elegant. Just the thing for you."

Faced with this opportunity to actually lead a life like Neil's – something I had wanted, or thought I wanted, for months – I held back. "Wouldn't I have to work evenings? What would I tell my family?"

"That it's a good job, pays well, but you have to work afternoons and evenings. Not implausible. You say you want to live like me; here's your chance. Are you interested?"

"I guess so, but I'm just a bit scared."

"Understandable."

"Were you, at first?"

"Of course, but I got over it. It was an adventure, and still is."

"What would I have to do?"

"First, be interviewed by Neddy. I'll set it up."

"What's he like?"

"Never mind. I think you'll get along."

AT THREE P.M. THE following day, dressed neatly in cap, jacket, and nut huggers, I was striding down Broadway, with its roar of stages and wagons and carts, shouts of drivers, and horses' hooves clattering on pavement stones. Arriving at the downstairs entrance of Young America, I paused: was I really going to do this? *Yes!* Up a flight of stairs I came to a door: YOUNG AMERICA MESSENGER & COURIER SERVICE: WE DELIVER THE GOODS, and in smaller print below, "Please enter." Spunking up my courage, I went in. Coming out was a good-looking boy who glanced at me and winked.

Inside I found a small room with several benches, a counter stacked with parcels and sealed envelopes, and on the wall a sign: QUALITY COUNTS. Behind the counter a man sat at a desk playing solitaire. Hearing me enter, he rose and came to the counter: a thin build, sloping shoulders, and a weathered face framed by tufts of jet-black sideburns, and a thick crown of hair that looked too dark, too neat. He could have been anywhere from fifty to seventy in age. His gray features, I suspected, were faintly tinged with rouge. He looked at me, smiled.

"Tommy Vaughan, I presume? Ah yes, beautiful, beautiful…Neil, the dear boy, hasn't exaggerated. We're off to a flying start." A dulcet voice, caressing; I rather liked it. "Now Tommy, you understand the nature of the … uh … services we provide?"

"Yes, sir."

"Of course you do, hee, hee. And you have no objections?"

"No, sir."

"Excellent. Now if you'll just follow me back to the viewing room…"

He raised a section of the counter, so I could pass behind it and follow him down a short passageway to a room in back. We entered; he closed the door. Having a skylight, the room was flooded with light. There was an ottoman with cushions, a hassock, a few chairs, and full-length mirrors on the walls. So far he'd done all the talking; it was strange, exciting.

"Now if you'll just remove your clothes, all of them, I'll have a – hee, hee – look-see. I, alas, shall keep mine on."

Neil had forewarned me; I did as instructed.

"There we go, good boy. Oh, very nice – better and better. Exquisite, exquisite. If you get an erection, so much the better, though given Neil's recommendation, I can take that – hee, hee – on faith. Ooh, the little rascal! Coming along, aren't we? Naughty, naughty! Oh, what a devil – all atingle for action, isn't he? Well, he'll get plenty. Now if you'll just turn around, so I can check out the other side. Oh, sublime! Peaches, but without the fuzz. We like fuzzies too, but smoothies are so in demand. Yes, dear boy, I shall call you 'Peaches.' You'd be surprised how many young youths pad themselves fore and aft, hence the need for a viewing. Not that I – hee, hee – mind, and neither, I suspect, do you. You may turn around again and face me. Ooh, he's still there, isn't he? Absolutely, positively brazen. Clearly, you'll do, you'll quite do. Lucky clients! Peaches, dear Peaches, you have gladdened me, you have fueled my fantasies for nights to come. I am humbly, oh so humbly, grateful, a spark of joy in my desiccated life. But bliss, alas, always has a term. You may put your clothes back on. If you can, that is. I shall – hee, hee – watch."

He did. By doing a quick bit of algebra – a favorite trick of mine – I got things under control and squeezed back into the huggers. It hadn't been so bad. He was funny; I was beginning to like him.

Back in the outer room I stood at the counter while he filled out a form.

"So we can describe you to the clients. Some of them are rather demanding when it comes to details. Five foot…?"

"Four."

"Perfect. Please don't grow any more, dear boy, you mustn't overtop the clients. Eyes: blue. Azure, the color of heaven. Hair: brown."

"Auburn."

"Quite so, auburn. Smooth, not hirsute, boyish. The cap and jacket are fine, by the way: a boyish look. As for the huggers, the less said the better. Not that they'll – hee, hee – stay on very long."

Looking at Mr. Neddy's withered features, in my mind I brushed away the wrinkles, replaced the ridiculous wig with a crop of thick black hair, and there before me was one of the prancing little poufs of the

Garden, pert, mincing, young, quite good-looking in a pouf sort of way, with a buoyant sense of humor that on occasion, I suspected, might turn tart and sting. Then the vision faded and I saw again the gray nance of today. Eerie.

He asked a few more questions: address, living with whom, education. Then with a flourish he put his pen down.

"There, dear boy, dear Peaches, I think that does it. We do try to match our boys with the clients – their needs, their desires – but while we provide your services for a stipulated amount of time, we don't guarantee specific acts; that's between you and the clients. You will of course be obliging. We'll screen out the cranks. We will never contact you at home. You will check in here daily, at exactly eleven a.m. – do be prompt -- to see if a client has requested you. You'll then go to his address at a specified time, and – hee, hee – marvelous things will happen. Twenty dollars for an hour, thirty for an evening, fifty for an overnight."

"I can't do overnight."

"I understand – the family. You'll bring us our share – half – at eleven the next day; we do insist on that. So for now, dear Peaches, good-bye. Look in tomorrow; I'm sure you'll have a client."

It had all been slightly unreal; I left.

WHEN I INFORMED MY family that I had a good job with the Young America Messenger & Courier Service on Broadway, working afternoons and evenings, starting in a day or so, Mother was thrilled.

"Now my dear boy is going to find out what the real world is like. Your father would be proud."

"What's so special?" asked Stewart. "I've been in the real world for years."

Two, to be exact.

THAT NIGHT I HAD a hassle of dreams. Waking, I thought of the Garden, then of Mr. Neddy's gray, withered features. Was I really going through with it? To cavort with Neil was one thing; to do it with a horde of strangers – and for money at that! – quite another. So maybe not. Then I thought of Neil, his adventures and his glittering clothes. Yes, maybe. No. Yes! No. No? No.

AT ELEVEN SHARP THE following morning I was in Mr. Neddy's office. The parcels and sealed envelopes on the counter hadn't budged one inch. Seeing me, he rose from his game of solitaire and greeted me.

"Ah, dear Peaches, this is your big day. I have something for you; your name is in the – hee, hee – book of life."

He gestured toward a large wall calendar behind his desk that I hadn't noticed the day before. In the big squares for each day were written names that, by squinting, I could just make out: Muscles, Blondie, Cuddles, Rod, Muffin, Teaser, and sure enough, scribbled in the one for that day in bold red ink, Peaches. Mr. Neddy gave me a slip of paper with a name and address.

"A Mr. Owen on Twenty-eighth Street; an importer, I believe. Uses our services regularly. Eight p.m.; be prompt. Any questions?"

"I don't think so. I've talked with Neil."

"Fine. That's it. Good luck! Bring the money tomorrow."

He blew a kiss, then went back to his cards.

AT EIGHT THAT EVENING, in cap, jacket, and huggers, I stood at the top of a stoop, before the frosted-glass double doors of an elegant brownstone on Twenty-eighth Street, pulling a silver-handled bell pull. Should I have knocked at the basement door underneath the stoop? Too late; I could hear the chime inside. I waited, heart pounding. Now at last I would enter that world of night that Neil resided in and I had only glimpsed, home of the sensual, the wild, the forbidden.

A shadowy form loomed behind the frosted glass of the doors; they opened. A man's voice: "Come in, come in."

I stepped in; he closed the door behind me. A short, plump man of fifty, his jowly features fringed with graying whiskers, in shirt sleeves and a dark waistcoat with a watch chain stretched across it.

"Tom, isn't it? You're punctual; that's good." He looked at me more closely. "Oh yes, quite satisfactory, quite. Come along now to my study."

Before I could say good evening, he started off; I followed. He led me down a corridor to a room in back with chairs, an ottoman with cushions, shelves with books, and a desk stacked high with papers and an open ledger.

"We'll do it here." He pointed to the ottoman. "Please take off your clothes."

"Everything?"

"Everything. I'll be with you in a minute."

"Your name, sir?" I knew it, but thought he ought to tell me.

"Owen. Jeffrey Owen."

"Glad to meet you, sir."

"Yes, yes."

I had a hunch that wasn't his real name, but no matter. He went back to the desk, sat, made entries in the ledger. I undressed, sat on the ottoman, waited. I felt awkward, exposed, almost silly; my dingus was limp.

For at least ten minutes he sat there, scanning some papers and furiously scribbling in the ledger: the kind of work, I thought, that ought to be consigned to a clerk. As he wrote, he clucked his tongue at times, shook his head, mumbled. Finally he glanced at his watch, put down his pen with a sigh.

"That should do for now."

He got up and, without ever looking at me, peeled off his clothes and piled them neatly on a chair. He wore a lace corset that astonished me; I didn't know men wore them. As he unlaced it, his flesh bulged out all over. He approached me.

"Let's get to it, shall we? First I'll do you, then you do me. All right?"

"That would be fine, Mr. Owen."

I lay back, wondering how I'd ever get it up.

"Just a minute." He hurried back to his desk, sat, made another entry in the ledger, came back. "Now where was I?"

"You were doing me, sir."

"So I was."

I lay back again. He started in; his flesh jiggled. By shutting my eyes and thinking of Neil, I managed to give him something to work with. Finally I got it off.

"Very satisfactory," he announced. "Your turn." He lay back.

Though hardly inspired, I did what was expected. To my surprise, it didn't take long.

"Nice, Sam. Very nice."

I didn't correct him. "Glad to oblige, Mr. Owen."

He sat up, reached for his watch. "We'd better get dressed."

We did. Watching him lace himself into that corset, I squelched a smile. Neil had warned me: never laugh at a client.

Finally he made it, got the rest of his clothes on, combed his hair. "Quite satisfactory, Sam. Here's your money."

"Thank you, Mr. Owen."

"I'll show you out."

At the door I said good-bye, got a quick glance cold as marble.

"Yes, yes." He shut the door.

Tool! I thought, as I skittered down the stoop.

THE NEXT MORNING NEIL waved me into his room, shut the door.

"How was it?"

"Ho-hum, bore-dom."

"That bad?"

"Worse."

"Tell me."

I told him.

"A cold fish," said Neil. "You'll get them. It can't be helped."

"He made me feel like a *thing*. And that corset – I couldn't believe it."

"Corsets, wigs, dentures – you'll see it all. You've got to take it in stride."

"I never dreamed vice could be so dull."

"Sometimes, not always."

"I need consolation."

"How's this?"

He kissed me, we fell into bed. Well into the lovemaking, I blurted out,

"The moment he got rid of me, I'll bet he went back to that ledger!"

Neil kept kissing me.

"Incidental expenses. Satisfaction: twenty dollars."

7

The next day, when I gave Mr. Neddy his money, I made it clear that my first contact had been less than radiant.

"Yes, dear Peaches, I've had several reports to that effect about him. Most regrettable. I'll try to do better next time. I have a learned gentleman in mind, well-traveled and urbane."

"That would be more like it."

"I'll see what I can do."

Coming away from the office, I ran into Metcalf on busy Broadway. I hadn't seen him since graduation. He looked dapper enough in his checked trousers and derby: a man about town on the prowl.

"Hi, kid, how's it going? Not too dull, I hope. I've been running wild. Did you know that you can have sex in this city any time, any place? In the past week I had an office boy in a cellar, a workman in an alleyway, a flash young guy in a closed carriage, and a policeman under a bush in the Park."

"How was it?"

"Smashing! But I don't recommend the carriage: too cramped. Or the Park either: mosquitoes."

He was ruddy-faced and radiant, brawny, solid, lithe.

"Aren't you supposed to be preparing for college?"

"God, yes. The old man wants me to be a doctor like him, and my grades aren't up to snuff. I'll hit the books one of these days. Right now I'm going to check out Washington Square; I've heard there's lots of action. High times in Sodom on the Hudson. See you!"

A quick smile; he was off.

THAT SAME WEEK WHEN I was developing sensually, Mother was aspiring to new heights spiritually. This, she hoped, would occur at a high tea sponsored by the Dames of Charity honoring her idol, Cora Worthington, the Sweet Singer of Hackensack, whose *Weeping Willow Songs* and *Balm for the Afflicted*, still lodged on Mother's bedside table, had long ago consoled her through her time of deep mourning for my father. Ever since then she had kept on a shelf beside her desk in the sitting room a slew of Miss Worthington's essays and advice books: *The Frugal House-wife, The Joyful Abstinence Cookbook, Whispers to a Bride, The Lady's Companion,* and *Mystic Womanhood*. Buoyant from intercourse with God, Miss Worthington never failed to remind her readers how, by scratching her pen on foolscap through long nights with a statue of the risen Christ before her, she had achieved a vision of a world where men would be more like women, and women more like angels: "We need radiant souls!"

In consequence, Mother professed to feel an inner radiance and, along with most of the Dames of Charity, had long since become a cheerful advocate of Miss Worthington's causes: universal peace, benign prisons, beverages that cheer but not inebriate, the City and House Beautiful, and broccoli. She quoted the noted authoress's sayings and stitched them into her needlework. To achieve the House Beautiful, Mother was constantly rearranging the furnishings of our parlor – she couldn't afford to buy new ones – and imposed on Stewart and me a steady diet of broccoli, which we both loathed; broccoli, according to Miss Worthington, attuned one to the Higher Harmony. Now at last Mother would meet this shining eminence, commune with her, and obtain her autograph in a new edition of *The Joyful Abstinence Cookbook*. She left in high hopes and came back radiant.

"So what's she like?" I asked.

"A soft soul shining. She has lovely hands."

Mother displayed the autograph with a flourish: "For dearest Susana, a kindred Soul, a seeker of Harmony, my sister in Peace. – Cora Worthington." I didn't point out that Miss Worthington had misspelled "Susanna."

"A pure spirit, if there ever was one," said Mother. "She has vowed never to utter or write a single word unmentionable to ears polite."

At dinner that evening Margaret set before us dishes heaped high with broccoli, spinach, and asparagus.

"Where's the meat?" asked Stewart.

"There isn't any, dear. Miss Worthington's new cookbook is entirely vegetarian. She says meat kindles the baser passions. A vegetarian diet benefits body, mind, and spirit."

Stewart flung his fork down with a clatter. "Mother, I want meat."

"Carnivorous societies are notoriously violent. Look at the terrible war this country just endured."

"Mother, I have a right to eat meat. It's in the Declaration of Independence: 'life, liberty, and the pursuit of meat.' "

"I'm sure I've never heard that, dear."

"He's right, Mother," I put in. "The Founding Fathers were great hunters and eaters of meat."

"Really?"

"Oh yes. Dr. Murdock said so."

"So you see, Mother," said Stewart, "as a freeborn American citizen

I have a right to eat meat. I don't care what that crazy woman says."

"She is a shining light!"

"Well she doesn't shine in *my* direction. I won't give up meat!"

"Hear, hear!" I said. For once, Stewart and I were in perfect agreement.

"So both my boys are against me. I'm sure I meant for the best."

She was tearing now, but to no avail; her tears had long since ceased to move us.

Mother accepted defeat gamely. Thereafter, while herself abstaining, she continued to serve us meat, albeit with heaping portions of broccoli. And that was that.

TWO DAYS LATER MR. Neddy informed me that I had another client.

"The well-traveled gentleman, learned and urbane?"

"No, he's out of town. This is a Mr. Thompson, a rising young lawyer on Centre Street, near the Tombs. Be at his office at seven-thirty tonight. You're – hee, hee – well rested, I assume?"

"Of course."

"Ah, the energy of youth! Dear Peaches, you may need it."

"Why?"

"Never mind."

THE ADDRESS WAS RIGHT across from the Tombs, that gloomy old building with a front portico of squat heavy columns, where cases were tried and hundreds of prisoners were locked in somber cells. Not the cheeriest beginning for an evening. Up two flights of stairs I came to a door with lettering: *Mark Thompson, attorney-at-law.* There was light inside; the rest of the floor was dark. I knocked.

"Come in!"

A man of about thirty-five with lustrous black hair, a thin, well-

trimmed mustache, no beard, in a frock coat and cravat. He met me at
the door, waved me in.

"Welcome, Tom, welcome to the Law. I'm Mark Thompson, services available to all for a price – something we have in common. Ever
been in a lawyer's office?"

"No, sir."

"Briefs, briefs, briefs. Writs, summonses, affidavits, be-it-knowns,
and whereases. It's coming out of my ears. So right here in this most
respectable building – we're the only ones here, I've made sure of it –
you, you little rascal, are going to snatch me away from these horrors."

The office had shelves lined with ranks of gray law books, a framed
diploma on the wall, a table piled high with red-taped files, chairs, a bust
on a pedestal marked CICERO, a desk with cubbyholes stuffed with
papers, and of course an ottoman. He took off his coat and shoes, loosened his cravat and tossed it on the desk, then looked at me. His voice
was strong and vibrant.

"You little devil, coming to me in those tight pants. Whatever is on
your mind?"

He was young, tight-knit, brash; suddenly I felt devilish. "Stud,
that's for me to know and you to find out."

He grabbed me. "Let's do dirties!"

In no time he stripped me to my underpants. "And now, you little
tease, I'm going to give you what-for!"

I stuck my tongue out at him. He pounced like a tiger, I dodged; he
chased me around the table. Finally he caught me, pressed me up against
the wall. I was giggling.

"You little punk, you catamite!" (A word I'd never heard.) "How's
this for a start?"

He kissed me. Wiggling and flailing my arms, I hit the framed diploma; it crashed to the floor.

"Whore, have you no respect for the Law?"

"Screw the Law!"

As he reached to retrieve the diploma, I wrenched free and darted across the room. Smirking, I paused there out of reach, while he tossed off his shirt and pants, snatched up a fly whisk, and came for me.

"I'm going to tan your buns!"

"You'll have to catch me first!"

He lunged, brushed against the files on the table; they spilled on the floor, pencils scattered.

"Punk, you're making a mess of my office!" He lunged again, grinning.

"Frig your office!"

As he chased me around the bust of Cicero, we jostled it; it fell. He caught it; heavy, it almost bore him to the floor. He thrust it back up on the pedestal.

"And frig Cicero!" I shouted, and stuck my tongue out again. I'd never felt like this; it was fun.

"You rowdy little slut, I'll get you!"

"Says who?"

As he chased me, I overturned chairs to block him. Finally I let him catch me at the door and carry me, kicking and squirming, to the ottoman. He snatched off my underpants, tossed them in the air; they landed on Cicero. Stripping himself buck naked, he held me prone on the ottoman. I felt deliciously helpless.

"And now I shall leave my mark on you!"

"No, please, no!" I was squirming.

I felt his teeth sink into my buttocks, first into one, then the other, just hard enough to leave an imprint.

"There! Try explaining *that* to your mother!"

"I can't! I'm so embarrassed!" I was tearing and giggling all at once.

"And now, the spanking!"

He lashed my buns with the whisk. It was only a whisk; it didn't hurt, I loved it. Then he flipped me over.

"Just as I thought! Punk, have you no shame, no modesty?"

"None, you dolt of a stud!"

"Then taste this!"

He did me; I came like thunder. I'd never been so excited in my life.

He watched me for a few minutes, grinning. Then: "You don't get off that easy." He shoved me to my knees; I started in.

"Don't be so prim and proper!"

He had me in a frenzy; I was noisy. When he spent, it was wondrously prime. Finally I got up and lay down on the ottoman beside him.

"You greedy little whore…" he whispered.

I looked at him, grinned, said nothing.

"Had enough?"

"No!"

We did it two more times.

Sated at last, we lay there side by side on the ottoman. Shivered into a thousand pieces, I was speechless, dazed, still aware of his body, its smell of musk and sweat.

Finally he sat up, looked around: "God, what a mess!"

With effort I sat up, looked: chairs overturned, clothes and loose files everywhere, my underpants on Cicero. Lurching to his feet, he put on his underwear and pants. I got up, too, retrieved my underpants, poked around in the litter for my other clothes, got dressed.

"I'll help you clean up," I offered.

We piled the loose files back on the table, set upright the overturned chairs. He straightened Cicero and hung his diploma back on the wall.

"Kid, you caught on fast."

"Well, it's been an experience."

"Boys inspire me. What a juicy little piece you are! I've half a mind to yank your britches down and spank you again."

"A bully thought, but I think we're both played out."

"You just might have a point."

"Not now, I don't. I couldn't."

We both giggled.

"Here's the money, kid; you earned it. There's a bonus. It's for you; don't split it with Neddy."

"Thank you, Mr. Thompson. It was wild."

He showed me to the door in his sock feet, slapped my behind, and sent me off. He had given me thirty dollars; twenty of it was mine — more than Stewart earned in a week.

Aunt Jessie had said that Neil never laughed. When I told him about the lawyer chasing me around his office, he laughed plenty, and when I mentioned my underpants on Cicero, he roared.

8

OVER THE NEXT TWO weeks I had a string of clients who just wanted basic servicing, but they were civil and remembered my name. To my regret, no further mention of the learned gentleman, well-traveled and urbane. But I was getting known. More and more often I saw "Peaches" scrawled in red on the calendar. I gave five dollars a week to Mother, and used the rest of my earnings to buy two more pair of nut huggers; they went over big with the clients.

Some clients called on me for matinées, but most of them wanted me at night. Only when immersed in darkness, by candlelight or with the lamps turned low, could they slough off conventions and restraints and fuel their fantasies; they reveled in the sperm-rich night. Yet no matter how well I satisfied them, few of them wanted to see me again. I asked Neil why.

"Lots of them just want a boy to come with, they don't care who. Others feel too much shame and guilt to see the same boy twice. And still others are looking for the Ideal Boy, the Perfect Experience; no matter how good you are, they'll never be completely satisfied. It's just as well. You don't want to get involved with a client. If you're good, word gets around. There'll always be more clients."

There always were.

"THIS WILL BE DIFFERENT, dear boy," Mr. Neddy informed me one Friday.

"The learned gentleman?"

"No, no, dear Peaches, he's still out of town, though due back any day. This will be different in another way."

"How do you mean?"

"You'll see soon enough. Just go to this address and do as you're told. I wouldn't send just anyone. No nut huggers this time. I trust to your discretion."

It was an address just off the upper Fifth Avenue, the city's most elegant thoroughfare, lined with handsome brownstone residences. When I got there at eight that evening, it proved to be the marble rectory adjoining the Church of Christ and All Angels, which shone through the dark with the illumined crystal cross on its steeple. The rectory: I was astonished. Was someone in the Reverend Blythe's household ripe for a romp? Inconceivable. I rapped the silver knocker, waited. The door opened.

"Come in, young man, come in."

Greeting me was the Reverend Timothy Blythe himself, tall, richly sideburned, smiling, in a dark lounging jacket with silk facings and a clerical collar. Over the years he had seen me dozens of times during pastoral visits in our parlor, always proclaiming me a "splendid little chap," but if he recognized me now, he gave no hint. This was going to be interesting.

I followed him down a carpeted hallway to his study: a spacious room with bookcases holding Bibles and other books in black bindings, stands with vases of roses, an ottoman with fringed blue cushions, and a red damask chair drawn up to an oak writing table littered with papers. Over the table, framed, in needlepoint: LOVE. In the air I detected a hint of incense, an aroma far subtler than the stuff my mother burned on special occasions in our parlor.

He drew me near a lamp on the desk, looked at me. "An angel…an angel come to earth!" His gray eyes gazed into mine. "Tom, is it not?"

"Yes, sir."

Still no trace of recognition. Little wonder: we both had a lot to lose.

"I'm still working on my sermon, Tom. Almost done. Pull up a chair. Maybe you can help."

He sat at the desk; I pulled up a chair. In front of him lay sheets of monogrammed paper, some scribbled over, some clean, with a jeweled paperweight and a silver-tipped pen.

"Just listen, Tom; I'm at the very end." He cleared his throat, then spoke in a resonant voice. "'Meek or bold, he evinced good manners. Neat, precise, well-groomed, never shabby, courteous, affable, accessible to all, he showed a rare gentility. The…the…the *what?* of the gentleman is Jesus.' Oh Tom, how I've sweated over that phrase! The *model* of the gentleman is Jesus? No. The *pattern…?* The *essence…?* No, no, no. So close, but not quite right. Help me, Tom. Help me!"

I thought. "Epitome."

"What?"

"Epitome."

"The *epitome* of the gentleman is Jesus." He pursed his lips, pondered, then brightened into a radiant smile. "Yes, Tom, yes! Brilliant! Absolutely brilliant! 'The *epitome* of the gentleman is Jesus.'"

He drew me to him and kissed me on the cheek. I noticed a big red ring on his finger, breathed the aroma of his scented silk handkerchief.

He inserted the word on the paper in front of him, then flung down the silver-tipped pen. "Done at last! What a relief!"

"Glad to be of help, sir." I was opting for "sir," since "reverend" didn't quite seem appropriate.

"Dear boy, dear Tom, will you join me in a glass of wine?"

"As you wish, sir. I'm at your service."

From a sideboard he fetched a decanter and two stemmed glasses, poured two half-glasses of red wine, offered me one.

"How I love that rich red color. Look, Tom, how the light shines through it. Liquid ruby – the color of the Holy Blood!"

He held his glass up in the light, gazed at it. Then he looked over at me. "I toast your beauty, Tom. You are an angel come to earth!"

He sipped the wine. His voice now was soft, seductive; it cast a spell. I sipped, too: aside from thimblefuls at Communion, the first wine I'd ever had. Like grape juice, yet different; I liked it.

"Taste it, Tom. Savor it. Feel how it lies like velvet on the tongue."

"Yes, sir. Ever so much subtler than beer."

"Good, Tom. Very good. It is the civilized drink and, of course, a sacramental one. Dull would life be without it."

In small sips we finished it. He stood up.

"And now the laying on of the hands."

His fingers stroked my face. He had a silken touch.

"Tom, oh Tom, how in the paths of darkness I have longed for light! At this moment you are a glimmer, a pure ray of that light."

"Yes, sir."

He turned down the lamp, lit two candles; through the semidarkness came a scent of pine.

"We are quite alone here in our sanctuary; I've arranged it. Tom, you will remove your clothes."

I did, silently, dropping them one by one on the carpet. Naked, I showed myself.

"Ah, the Elevation…!"

Was he serious? Dead serious.

"And now, dear boy, I shall lead you beside still waters."

Grasping my organ gently but firmly, he led me to the inevitable ottoman. There, as I stood facing him, he ran his hands down my flanks, caressed me.

"Behold, thou art fair, my love; thou hast dove's eyes."

Well, they were blue, but anyway…He kissed me.

"His lips are like lilies dropping sweet-smelling myrrh."

Myrrh or not, by now his mood was getting to me; I was really excited. He pressed me down on the ottoman, then slipped out of his own clothes with amazing speed. Thank God, no corset. His *membrum virile* was impressive.

"Dear boy, I shall taste of your flesh and your wine."

Did he ever! His gray head bobbed gently before me; I got there in no time at all. Around me in the shadows, the pine scent of the flickering candles mingled with the perfume of the roses and a trace of cologne from his body. I was vastly at peace.

"And now, dear boy…"

He stood before me; I began. It went fast.

"Glory…!" he whispered.

I held very still, then rose quietly and joined him on the ottoman. For a few minutes we lay there in silence.

"Such sweet communion! I needed that, Tom, dear Tom. Oh how I needed it!"

He had seduced us both. No matter; for his touch alone I would have forgiven him anything.

"Tom, try to understand. Once or twice a year I crave it. Bless you, my boy, bless you. You have given me bliss."

The benediction. His sermons were gilded platitudes, deftly delivered; here he was speaking from the heart. We both sat up.

"Tom, so few understand. Desire is holy. Will you remember that, Tom?"

"Yes, sir," I whispered. "Desire is holy."

"God bless you, dear sweet boy."

He turned the lamp back up; we found our clothes, got dressed. He handed me a scented envelope.

"This, Tom, is for you. I thank you for one of the most beautiful experiences of my life. I thank you humbly."

"Yes, sir. Much obliged."

"And please take this, too."

From a whatnot he took a pink seashell inscribed with something printed in gold and pressed it into my hand.

"Thank you, sir. It's beautiful."

We were still whispering; to have done otherwise would have seemed like sacrilege.

He led me back down the hallway to the door. There he kissed me again.

"The kiss of peace. Good-bye, Tom. Bless you."

"Good-bye, sir. God be with you."

When, outside, I heard the door close softly behind me, I felt like I was waking from a dream. In the envelope was forty dollars – a fortune! I'd never had forty dollars in my life.

I TOLD NO ONE, not even Neil, of this experience. When I went to church with Mother on Sunday, it was only when I heard him pronounce at the end of the sermon, "The epitome of the gentleman is Jesus," that I could really, truly grasp that this splendidly gold-robed priest, so impressive against the white marble altar, was the same man who had loved me two nights before. I had been to a secret place in his soul that no one else – not his wife and servants, his bishop, the churchwardens, the vestrymen, the choir, the congregation – had ever been to or even knew existed. "Desire is holy": those words would long echo in my mind. After the service he greeted parishioners at the entrance, its Gothic arch topped by carved trumpeting angels. When our eyes met, blue against gray, he still gave no sign of recognition. Was he a prince of deceit or a master of oblivion? I couldn't tell. It was the beginning of a long game between us.

Inscribed in gold on the seashell was the Lord's Prayer, which seemed strangely fitting, though I couldn't say why. I presented it to Mother, explaining that I had received it for services rendered as a messenger. She found it "utterly charming, so delicate, so inspiring, quite conducive to the Higher Harmony," and displayed it on a whatnot in the parlor, where I hoped the donor might spot it in the course of his next pastoral visit.

9

I HAD LOTS OF clients now. Some, the moment they had spent, hustled into their clothes, ordered me to do the same, and sent me packing; I hated them. But others begged me to spend the night with them and were eager to pay extra for it; it annoyed me that I couldn't. So Mr. Neddy and I worked out a plan. From time to time I would inform my family that I was needed on a posting to Hartford or Providence or Trenton, where Young America would lodge me in a hotel overnight; for these assignments I would of course be amply paid. Mother welcomed this sign of my advancement and the additional income it would bring; Stewart said nothing. So I bought a carpetbag and tossed into it on these occasions a toothbrush, nightclothes (rarely needed), a change of linen, and the indispensable huggers. If Mother asked about the cities I visited, I told her that my schedule left no time for seeing the sights; my diligence impressed her.

In this way I came at last to really know night and the glories of a full night of love: the delicious alternation between a lover's clasps and probings, and stretches of sweet sleep, followed by another bout of love; the sleeping spoons with a lover, locked in his arms; the summons, in a strange hotel room or town house, to a late-morning breakfast, my clothed lover insisting that I come to the table naked, so he could feast his eyes on me as I sipped tea and munched muffins, only to be yanked back to bed. From these revels I emerged tired, dazed, groggy, wincing at the noonday sun and the brisk pace of shoppers, their business still before them, while I drooped homeward, craving only a long sleep deep into the waning day, from which I finally wakened, well rested, feeling lazy and languorous, my whole body tingling with the return of desire.

EARNING MORE, WITH NEIL'S guidance I spent more money on clothes: velvet slippers, patterned waistcoats, silk cravats, and black shoes with chic pointed toes. Since I didn't wear these items at home, Mother and Stewart, who never came to my room, hadn't noticed, but once I found Margaret eyeing the array of my wardrobe.

"Oh Master Thomas, such foine new things you have! You must be doin' well on that job."

"Yes, Margaret, I'm doing well and I like nice things. But let's not mention them to Mother or Stewart. Stewart would be fearfully jealous."

"That he would, Master Thomas, that he would. He'd raise a foine rumpus for sure."

I slipped her a dollar; her lips were safely sealed.

IN ALL SUCH MATTERS Neil was my counselor; I saw him almost daily. Sometimes we even showered together, which usually ended in a dash to his room for a romp. Finally he decreed that we should limit our frolics to at most once a week, so as not to be depleted for the clients; reluctantly I had to agree. We didn't think of ourselves as lovers; it was just rambustious fun.

Together, Neil and I drew up a set of rules for ourselves. What started as a joke turned into a serious endeavor.

THE TEN COMMANDMENTS OF MALE PROSTITUTION AS PRACTICED IN THIS CITY
by two who know

1. Accept whatever name the client gives you; never give him your own last name.

2. Always laugh at a client's jokes, but never at his drawers, corset, dentures, or wig; always compliment him on the size and thrust of his apparatus, no matter how lamentably small.

3. Do not show yourself around too often; appear desirable but almost inaccessible.

4. Don't smoke; it taints the breath.

5. Drink only one glass of spirits a day with a client; you must remain lucid and observant, even if he does not.

6. No beard or mustache; always look boyish.

7. No erections in public.

8. If you see a client in church, do not accost him; if he smiles, winks, or otherwise acknowledges you, nod civilly.

9. In public, allow one pinch per buttock only, and never on the street; no groping whatsoever.

10. When pinched in private, always squeal; it excites the client and gives him a feeling of power.

Hearing of our rules, Mr. Neddy asked for a copy, printed them up, and distributed them to all of his boys. Neil and I felt that we had made a real contribution to the trade.

"DEAR PEACHES, I HAVE a new client for you, the learned gentleman."

"Well-traveled and urbane?"

"Exactly. He's back in town. I've mentioned you to him, and he's quite eager to meet you. But be warned: you may need patience for this one."

By now I knew better than to question Mr. Neddy further. He would always say just enough to pique my curiosity, but nothing more.

At seven that evening I was pulling the bell pull of a handsome brownstone on East Eighteenth Street. The door was opened by a man in his forties with a well-trimmed mustache and goatee, and long, slightly graying sideburns, wearing a lounging jacket and tie.

"Good evening, Tom. Come in. I am Walter Whiting."

"Good evening, sir."

A quick handshake, then he led me down a long corridor to a well-lit room in back.

"This is my study. I think we'll be comfortable here." A rich voice, with warmth; I liked it.

Books and prints lay about everywhere, amid a musty smell of old bindings. There were huge maps on the walls, a bust of Shakespeare on a mantel, a cluttered desk, of course an ottoman, and on a small stand beside it, a statuette of a rather fetching naked young man. The room looked more intensely lived in, less arranged and exquisite, than the Reverend Blythe's study. To know this room was to know, or begin to know, the occupant, who was certainly learned and well-traveled, and surely urbane, too.

"Come over here, Tom, so I can look at you."

I was used to this. I went over and stood in the light from a lamp; he gazed at me intently.

"The unbearable beauty of boys...!"

I said nothing, let him look.

"Here's the money, Tom. Let's get that out of the way right now."

He handed me an envelope; I pocketed it.

"Thank you, sir."

"Don't you want to count it?"

"Oh no, sir. I trust you."

"Fine. So let's sit down and talk. Why don't you take that hassock? I'll move Ganymede."

He picked up a large print lying on a hassock, waved me to a seat there.

"Did you say Ganymede, sir? I'd like to see it."

"You would? In that case, here it is."

I sat down; he handed me the print. It showed a statue of another naked youth, beardless, slender, subtly feminine.

"I've been called a Ganymede more than once. I never knew what the word meant. Who was he, sir?"

"Ah, the value of a classical education! In Greek myth Ganymede was the most beautiful boy in the world. So beautiful that Zeus, the ruler of gods and men, was smitten. Assuming the shape of an eagle, he snatched the boy away to Olympus, to be cupbearer of the gods. A Roman statue, copied from a lost Greek original."

"Wow, that's quite a story! Then it's a compliment, if someone calls you a Ganymede?"

"It certainly is."

"Still, I don't see much of a resemblance."

"I do. Smooth skin, slim build, almost feminine grace, and of course thin wrists."

Standing over me, he reached out and with the thumb and fingers of one hand easily circled my wrist. I liked the gesture, having always been proud of my slender frame, so different from the beefy, hairy torsos of the sturdies, with their bulging muscles.

"Shall I take my clothes off, sir?" I thought it was time for the ottoman.

He retrieved the print, stepped back. "No! You must understand,

Tom, that with me things aren't so simple. Let's talk a bit first."

"Oh. May I ask, sir, what kind of work you do? This room rather fascinates me, with all its maps and books and pictures."

He sat on a chair, with me at his feet on the hassock, an arrangement I rather liked.

"I'm a scholar and critic. I write books, give lectures. My areas of greatest interest are Greek and Roman antiquity, the Italian Renaissance, and English poetry of every period."

"That's impressive, sir. Do you teach?"

"I do not. I learned long ago that I am not temperamentally suited to facing a classroom of surly and obstreperous boys who yawn, doze, or whisper dirty stories to one another, while I beat my brains out trying to enlighten them. Instead, I have given my life to art and literature. They are my religion. 'Beauty is truth, truth beauty, -- that is all we know on earth...'"

"*Ye*, sir, not *we*."

"What?"

"That line from Keats goes, 'That is all *ye* know on earth, and all *ye* need to know.' "

He gave me a sharp look, went over to a bookcase, pulled out a volume, leafed through it, read.

"You're right. Good God, I've been misquoting it for years. And I thought I knew the 'Ode to a Grecian Urn' by heart."

"'Ode *on* a Grecian Urn,' sir."

"That's what I said."

"No, sir, you said '*to* a Grecian Urn.' We studied it at Dr. Murdock's Academy. He was very particular about such things."

"To the point of nitpicking, it would seem. Tom, I'm a scholar of some renown. I take exception to these petty criticisms. Suppose we change the subject."

"Yes, sir."

"Mr. Neddy recommends you highly. He says you're from a good family and educated, which indeed seems to be the case. For a boy in this…uh…profession, that is somewhat surprising. May I ask how you got into it?"

"I like being looked at by men. I like to pleasure them. And of course I like nice things."

"Hmm. May I ask why Mr. Neddy calls you 'Peaches'?"

"You can't guess, sir?"

"I cannot."

"Well, he likes my bottom."

"Yes, the old lecher would. Quite an ogler, I'm sure."

"Not that I mind, sir."

"No, I suppose you don't. Granted, that feature of the male anatomy is not to be disdained. It had its role to play in *amor socraticus*, which translates as –"

"Socratic love."

"So you've had Latin, too."

"Oh yes, sir. Four years."

"You continue to surprise me. But I doubt if old Murdock told you much about that kind of love."

"He mentioned the 'shameless lusts of Greece,' nothing more."

"Typical."

"What was it, sir?"

"Love between two boys, or between a man and a boy. Preferably the latter."

"I should think so. Boys lack maturity. But a man and a boy, *that* makes sense."

"I'm glad you think so. But tell me, how long have you been in this life?"

"With Mr. Neddy, you mean? Just a few months, though it seems like a year."

"It doesn't ever disgust you?"

"Oh no, sir. I'm giving pleasure. That's what I'm meant to do."

"Aren't some of your clients…well…ugly?"

"Faces can be ugly; all cocks are beautiful."

"You're very candid."

"But they are. I love cocksucking; don't you? And I'm good at it; everyone says so. I'm an absolutely first-rate cocksucker. I'd like to show you."

He sprang to his feet and paced up and down. "I've been in this game since before you were born, but I've never heard anyone, man or boy, who had an ounce of breeding, as you presumably do, bandy those words about so casually! It offends me."

"But sir, it's such a beautiful thing, cocksucking."

"You have this angelic countenance, you quote Keats and know Latin, and out of your mouth come these rank obscenities. It's…unsettling!"

"Sorry, sir."

"And you're so damned polite! Stop 'sirring' me; call me Walter."

"I can't do that, sir. Not yet."

"Why not?"

"Because we haven't been intimate. I'm younger than you. It would be presumptuous. Sir, if I mustn't say 'cocksucking,' what should I say?"

"Nothing, preferably. But if you must, say 'fellatio.' "

"I'd better write that down. Do you have a pen and paper, sir?"

"Are you serious?"

"Oh yes, sir."

Puzzled, he looked hard at me. "Yes, I believe you are." He fetched a pen and a pad of paper from his desk.

"Thank you, sir. Now if you'd just spell that word…And Gany-mede, too, by the way."

He spelled them; I wrote.

"And regarding the back-door approach, what should I say, if I'm not keen on being fucked?"

"Say, 'I don't care for anal intercourse.'"

"Oh. That's easy enough, but I'll write it down, too, while I'm at it. Thank you, sir."

"You're quite welcome."

I had had difficult clients before; I was determined to cope with this one. "Sir, shouldn't we get on with things? Fellatio, I mean." I flashed my most winsome smile. "I'll bet you've got a beaut."

"What are you talking about?"

"You know."

"No, I do not."

"Your *membrum virile*, your cock. I'll bet you've got a whopper."

He sprang to his feet again and paced. "You are the most brazen little whore I've ever known! You punk! You catamite!"

"Catamite, sir?"

"A catamite is a passive young boy who sells his body to men."

"Oh. Of course, that's why I'm here."

"Not any more, you aren't! Get out!"

I couldn't believe it; no client had ever kicked me out. I got up. "You really want me to leave, sir?"

"*Yes!*"

Now I was angry, too: *kicked out!* I fished in my pocket for the envelope with the money and flung it on his desk. Then I made straight for the door, hoping I could find my way out.

"Tom," he called, "come back!"

I stopped in the doorway, waited.

"Don't leave, Tom. Please come back."

I went back and sat on the edge of the hassock. "Mr. Whiting, you are very difficult."

He sat down wearily in his chair. "Yes, I am difficult. I apologize. All my life I've been struggling to accept myself, fighting prejudice, coming to terms with shame and guilt, and tying myself in knots all the while. Then here you come along skipping blithely, dancing sunshine and joy all over, with the face of an angel, sweet sixteen —"

"Seventeen, sir. Close to eighteen."

"Stop correcting me!" he shrieked, then calmed himself. "...sweet seventeen, up to your ears in depravity, and spouting obscenities like garden party chitchat. I confess that I resent it."

"I'm sorry, sir."

"And you're so damned polite!" He put his face in his hands for a moment, then suddenly looked up at me. "Holy God, why am I telling you this? You, of all people!"

"I don't know, sir, but I'll listen."

"You've listened enough for today. Please go."

"As you wish, sir."

We both got up. He retrieved the money from the desk, gave it to me.

"But sir, we never made it to the ottoman."

"We've done plenty. I've taken your time."

I pocketed the money. "Thank you, sir."

"For what? The money?"

"No, sir. For Ganymede, fellatio, *amor socraticus*, anal intercourse, and catamite. I'll have to write that last one down."

"You never cease to surprise me."

"Will I see you again, sir? Maybe when things get calmer? I'd like to."

"I don't know. I'm having trouble adjusting to your candor. Please go."

So I went.

WHY HAD I NEEDLED him? Though it went against my instincts, I could easily have stopped "sirring" him and, with effort, called him Walter. I suspected that I'd never see him again, and regretted it. Not the pleasantest of my clients – far from it – but interesting. His study offered a world I wanted to explore. And he was the only client who had ever really talked to me, and briefly even listened. Well, if he was out of my life almost as soon as he'd come into it, things would surely be smoother. Mr. Urbane and Well-Traveled was trouble, and who needs that?

10

"YOU HAVE BEEN SPECIFICALLY requested, dear Peaches, and much may come of it. Go to the Fifth Avenue Hotel at five this afternoon and ask for Mr. Blaise Montclair. He thinks he knows you."

I hadn't the foggiest notion who Blaise Montclair might be, but, dressed for action, I did as instructed. This was my first visit to the hotel, an elegant white-marble edifice at Twenty-Third Street, whose lobbies were thronged with visitors and, in the evening, with money men from Wall Street who gathered there to gossip and plant rumors.

Directed to room 509, I rode in the vertical railroad that had created such a sensation when the hotel opened on the eve of the war. It was an eerie experience, rising so quickly and smoothly in this dark shaft where, should the cables snap, you would plummet to certain death; but of course no cables snapped. Getting out on the fifth floor, I trod soundlessly on thick carpeting down the hallway, knocked at 509. The door was opened by a man of forty in a morning coat with a gold-rimmed monocle and a fiercely waxed imperial.

"Tommy boy, dear Tommy, it is indeed you — marvelous, marvelous!"

It was the Count, whom I hadn't seen in over a year. He bounded forward, kissed me on both cheeks, and drew me into the room, a spacious parlor with crystal chandeliers. A servant closed the door.

"Good afternoon, sir. What a surprise!"

"Let me look. Yes, yes, I remember: auburn hair, pert nose, sensual lips. But virgin no more: no, no, no, no, no; I can tell. Tommy boy is flying – flying high. Good! I say to Mr. Neddy I must have boy – no street boy, someone nice. He tell me Peaches: boy with bottom like peaches, no fuzz, a smoothie: I excite. I tell him, 'This I must see.' He say 'Tommy'; I wonder: is this marvelous boy I met at Lust Garden one year ago? No, such luck I cannot have. But it is! Adorable Tommy is Peaches – I excite!"

He kissed me again, this time on the lips, and pinched my bottom. My first kiss – and pinch – from a monocle.

"But Count, what happened to Danny?"

"Danny, dear Danny – sad story. I tell."

He drew me over to a plush sofa; we sat.

"Danny and I, we cross continent by diligence, very slow, very bumpy, see plains, buffles, cowboys, mountains, Indians. But in San Francisco he leaves me for mining baron. Fake count loses real boy to fake baron. Joke: ha, ha." He looked on the verge of tears.

"I'm sorry, sir."

"Danny was so nice. He say, 'Count, I like you, but soon you go back to Europe and I stay here. For Danny, no more Count. I must be practical, must think of future. Good-bye, Count. I remember you always.' He goes with mining baron; I cannot blame. So I come back by train – wonderful new transcontinental railroad – see Indians, mountains, cowboys, buffles, plains. Indian boys handsome, wear almost nothing. Cowboys handsome, too. But I am sad: no Danny."

"I'm really very sorry, sir."

"Well, boys come, boys go. Now I am again in New York, sail for Europe in just one week. What to do? Forget Danny, have good time. Dear Tommy, dear Peaches, I arrange with Mr. Neddy. We have good time together. You are my kept boy for one week, no?"

I was thrilled. "I am your kept boy for one week, *yes!*"

He flashed a broad smile; his monocle twinkled in the light. "Come! We start right now!"

He pulled me into a bedroom with a huge four-poster and windows with crimson brocade drapes. Clothes flew off in all directions; he had me on my tummy on the bed, kissing my bottom like crazy.

"Peaches, yes, peaches: adorable! I gobble up. Is gift from God, your bottom. No sacrilege. It brings joy."

By this time he had got me all spunked up, I was twisting and squirming on the counterpane, my face in a scented pillow. In no time I shot – right there on the blue silk counterpane. I was embarrassed.

"Oh Tommy, dear excitable boy! Is waste of spunk; you should have saved for *me*. Such is passion, dear, dear boy. Now I give *you* spunk."

He rolled me over and offered it; I knew what to do. Then, and for the whole week following, he got me so randy that I gave him whatever he wanted. And he wanted a lot.

After a flying trip home to grab my carpetbag, report to Neil, and inform Mother that a sudden assignment, very important, would take me away for several days, I was back at the hotel with the Count. Over dinner in the hotel's sumptuous dining room, he sketched out our agenda.

"Tonight, more love; I cannot get too much. Since Danny, I am starved. You, dear Peaches, are feast. Tomorrow and every day, shops in morning, Park in afternoon; I have rented carriage. To be seen with beautiful boy in Park, that for me is bliss. And we explore. I love New York, is always more to see. This hotel – vertical railroad goes up and down. Never had I dreamed such a thing: marvelous! So much to see, to do. What you show me, dear boy? Tell!"

I thought a minute. "The docks." Stewart had taken me there once years back, to show me where "real" boys went for excitement.

"Oh? What is there?"

"Shipyards, longshoremen, ocean liners, oyster boats, and if we're lucky, street boys swimming naked in the river."

"Ooh, naked boys in river; I excite. And visit Wall Street, and Battery for view of harbor. And dance at Lust Garden, dine at Delmonico's. And Saturday night, big party. Sunday we say good-bye; Monday I sail. We have fun, no?"

"We have fun, yes."

So began my whirlwind week with the Count.

MORNINGS WE SPENT IN the stores, where he bought walking sticks and cravats, silk handkerchiefs, a fawn derby, gloves of every color, a gold watch chain, tiepins, scarf pins, studs. His supply of funds seemed inexhaustible; I marveled at how the clerks fussed over him, straining to meet his every need. In the process he showered me with gloves, a silver tiepin, a tasseled walking stick; I could hardly refuse.

In the afternoons we drove in the Park, where our shiny black caleche, poised springily on four thin wheels, top down, with a liveried coachman on the box in front, outshone all but the fanciest rigs. Mixing in with the parade of carriages, we passed groves and gardens, a gushing fountain, lawns with peacocks and grazing sheep, and a vast reservoir that seemed like a sea. We were noticed; people nodded to us, we nodded back.

"Total strangers — I do not know," he confided to me with a chuckle. "Is money. They smell my money, nod. Ha, ha, joke. They think you my son. Also joke: ha, ha."

Dressed at my insistence more soberly – plain clothes, no jewelry in sight – we toured the docks on foot, with the coach following discreetly at a distance. In these rough quarters where strangers might invite insults or theft, I hoped we'd pass for an importer making a sortie from his counting house, accompanied by his confidential clerk. We saw towering cranes loading and unloading ships; cattle being prodded up a gangplank; steamboats coming and going; huge heaps of lumber, bricks, and coal; and scores of workers crawling over a ship's hull and pegging at it with hammers in drydock.

"Is marvelous!" he exclaimed. "New World zest and vigor. I am Old World, ancient, tired. This is Go Ahead. This is world of future!"

And when we saw scores of boys splashing about naked in the river, he almost popped his monocle. "Ah, youth! Such freedom! Such energy! Oh to be in there with them, laughing, splashing, groping, but alas, this cannot be. But I have you, dear Tommy: Young America. You deliver goods. Ha, ha."

He kept on looking. It was quite a while before I could pull him away.

BY MIDWEEK I MADE a point of going home for dinner and the night, so as to allay any family suspicions. But I would be off again tomorrow, I explained.

"Poor Tom," said Mother. "They're working you so hard. This job must be a real ordeal."

"Mmm."

The next morning, before leaving, I managed to connect with Neil. When I first told him about the Count's proposal, he had warned me that this city drew every kind of humbug and bunco artist, so he'd better check this fellow out. Now he made his report.

"Whoever he is – and no one really knows – his money is good. He pays his bills, has credit all over the country."

"So he's as rich as he seems?"

"Apparently. No one knows his real name or where his money comes from, except maybe, just maybe, his banker. But who cares? You've got a good thing, Tom. Stick with it."

I did. I never learned exactly what arrangements the Count had made with Mr. Neddy, but I was guaranteed twenty dollars a day clear, plus dinners and frills: gloves, tiepins, walking sticks, and the like. And that wasn't all.

"This, Tommy, is for you," he said one afternoon, handing me a slender volume. "Is poetry of Mr. Whitman: manly love of comrades. I mention it a year ago, do not give, but do not forget. Is known in Europe already. You will read it, no?"

"I will read it, yes. Thank you, Count."

"Mr. Whitman I would like to meet, but do not know where he lives; not here, not now. Pity. Democratic man, unique. Read it after I go. Now, no time. I keep you busy."

Poetry, on top of everything else. I'd never had it so good.

BY LATE AFTERNOON THE Count and I would be back in his luxurious hotel suite, with its parlor, bedroom, dressing room, and bathing room. We showered, romped, napped, then bestirred ourselves lazily in anticipation of dinner and maybe dancing at the Garden. His valet Anton, quiet, efficient, poised, was always there like a scented shadow, ministering to his needs. At first I was uneasy in Anton's presence; the Count noticed.

"Tommy boy, little Peaches, do not worry about Anton. He is my other self, with me many years. He sees all, says nothing. He is musical, too." ("Musical" was the latest code word.)

I soon got used to Anton and his quiet movements, soft voice, all but forgetting he was there. He practiced invisibility.

THE COUNT'S TALK FASCINATED me; it shifted with his moods.

"Funny world, Tommy. I do not know your last name; you do not know my name at all. Blaise Montclair – fake name. And I am not real count. Yet we are friends, no?"

"We are friends, yes."

"So: I tell you funny stories."

He had a host of them, as well as strange lore acquired on his travels.

"In France nuns worship Sacred Prepuce. Is foreskin of Jesus, only part not ascended to heaven, long lost, now rediscovered. Think of it, Tommy. Catholic nuns worship Sacred Prepuce of Jesus! Who else think of that? What next? Sacred Navel? Sacred Toenails? Sacred Earwax? Those Catholics, they never miss trick!"

HE WAS CONTINUALLY AMAZED at the money men who gathered in the lobby downstairs.

"Every night they are there: babble, babble, babble. Never stop talking or thinking about money. That is America. When Commodore Vanderbilt, richest man in country, arrives, crowd makes way before him. In Europe we bow and scrape to princes; here you bow to wealth and power. America!"

HIS MOOD COULD CHANGE abruptly.

"Tommy, I have many pals, no friends. Pals love my money, not me. In each city I find one friend, my boy. I hire him but still he is friend, loyal until I leave. Here, Tommy, you are my only friend."

"I'm flattered, sir, but that's rather sad."

"Yes, is sad."

OCCASIONALLY HE WOULD GIVE hints as to where he was from.

"Tommy, I come from very distant land, very ancient."

"Really, sir?" I was curious but didn't want to pry.

"Vast plains, mighty mountains, thick forest. Like this country. But I cannot live there free, cannot have boys, so I travel. I go back once every year or two, so steward does not cheat me too much. I look at account books, smile or frown, leave. I have no home. Home is wherever I am. Right now it is here, with you." He reached over and tousled my hair. "Tommy, you are messenger. You bring me message of joy."

HE TALKED SO MUCH and let others talk so little, it seemed like he was afraid to let anyone else speak, afraid they might take over. I didn't mind; my talk could never have been as interesting as his.

"Tommy, in every city I go, I find new boy. Paris, Berlin, Munich, Amsterdam, Vienna: always, new boy. Leave city, leave boy. Always need new boy, always. Why?"

"What are you looking for, sir?"

"Yes – what? Boys, boys, boys, never enough. Maybe someday I get religion. No joke; serious. Maybe Jesus is beautiful boy. Maybe him I love – someday. Maybe."

Another time he confided, "In every city I change name. New city, new name, new boy. No one knows me."

"What are you afraid of, sir?"

"Good question, Tommy. What am I afraid of? Always I flee. Why?"

When I didn't know what to say to him – those rare moments when he seemed to want an answer – I smiled my most radiant smile. He called it my "angel smile." It got me off many a hook.

ON FRIDAY HE TOOK me to Wall Street. There was a huge speculation under way; someone was attempting the unheard-of: to corner gold.

Gold was soaring; stocks were plunging; the newspapers reported business paralyzed in every major city in the country. A block away from the Gold Room, the carriage was stopped by a hubbub of top-hatted men who were milling about in the street, shouting, gasping, gesticulating, while high up on a building nearby an outdoor indicator blazoned the price of gold: 150…155…160…With each rise, the crowd gave a roar. We watched from the open carriage in amazement, as men screamed, cursed, wept.

"What is happening? I do not understand. Do you understand, Tommy?"

"No, sir."

"They corner gold. They buy certificates – flimsy paper, not gold. Where is gold? Hidden somewhere? Why do they do this, why? Money, always money. America is money game; I do not understand."

"They're speculators, sir. That's all I know. Some win, some lose."

Suddenly the indicator flashed 155…150…145…The corner, it seemed, had been broken. The crowd had peaked to a frenzy, some laughing hysterically, some shouting curses and threats at we didn't know who or what. In the street nearby, a well-dressed man in a frock coat was weeping and hitting his forehead with his fist.

"Why? Why? Why?" Shaking his head, the Count told the coachman to turn back. "Is madness. Now we get out of hubbub. Now we find sanity and calm."

As we drove away, the crowd gave out roar after roar; gold was still plummeting. Gradually the noise faded behind us.

"Tommy," he said as we headed up Broadway, "tonight we dine at Delmonico's. No nut huggers, naughty boy, Delmonico's very correct, very formal. I cannot take fallen woman there, but I can take fallen boy. Very funny, ha, ha. But you are not fallen, dearest Peaches, you soar. Tonight wear nice formal trousers, frock coat, cravat. We dine with elite, no?"

"We dine with elite, yes."

THAT EVENING WE DINED at the Delmonico's on Fourteenth Street in a vast room lit softly with gaslight from crystal chandeliers, the tall windows framed with drapes of green damask. Waiters circulated noise-lessly on deep-pile carpets, amid a faint murmur of conversation from diners at tables bright with flowers, on whose white linen cloths crystal and silver gleamed.

The menu was in a French that baffled my modest ability; the Count ordered with ease: a thick, creamy soup for both of us, followed by woodcock with artichoke for him, and truffled roast chicken with spin-ach for me. The dishes were set before us at measured intervals, effort-lessly, as if by magic. The soup was tasty, my spinach velvety; the truffled chicken was permeated with an earthy mushroom savor to die for. His dessert was a peach compote; I had something called a baba au rhum, a rum-soaked sponge cake topped by whipped cream with a cherry in the center: delicious. I had never dined like this.

In that refined atmosphere no one gawked, but I was sure that we were noticed. Did they think I was his son? I wanted to whisper – no, shout – to that whole roomful of genteel diners, "He's keeping me and I love it! I'm his boy. Do you hear? I'm his boy!"

FOR SATURDAY NIGHT THE Count had planned a big party. He showed me the invitation he had sent out. It was engraved in gold lettering on cream-colored paper.

Count Blaise Montcalm de Montclair
cordially invites you
to a celebration of his love of this city

and farewell gala on the eve of his departure

7 p.m., Saturday, September 25, 1869

at the Albemarle Hotel

Broadway and Twenty-Fourth Street

catered by Delmonico's

featuring a *gâteau pyramidé*

"Sir, what's a *gâteau pyramidé*?"

"That, dear boy, is you. Before leaving city, I make you famous. Dear Peaches, you will be legend."

"What do you mean, sir?"

"I tell you later. Yes, Tommy Peaches is going to be legend."

And that's how it began: the weirdest episode of my career.

11

"DEAR TOMMY, HERE IS plan. I love this city, want to celebrate it. And I am leaving. No one gives me gala farewell, so I give it to myself, invite others. Good lesson in life, dearest boy: if no one honors you, honor yourself. Ha, ha."

"But what about me and the cake, sir?" We were lounging in his suite.

"I come to that. Engraved invitations go out to best musical circles – genteel people, no riffraff. Party is not here – too busy, too noisy. Is at Albemarle Hotel, more quiet and cozy, less noticed. In one room I offer big buffet catered by Delmonico's: lobster mayonnaise, roast snipe, truffled grouse, plus fancy vegetables and salad and of course champagne, much champagne. Everyone say, 'Count, we are here; where is Tommy?' I say, 'Tommy will join us, never fear.' Puzzlement, suspense. Then I invite them into other room. There, on table, is huge pyramided cake in seven tiers, all covered over with icing: work of art. They gather round, ooh and aah, are eager to consume. I take knife to cut, say magic word, and out of cake bursts lovely naked boy: you."

"Me?"

"You. You are hidden in cake and at signal burst out. Astonishment, applause. They gobble you with eyes, then gobble cake. Is climax of evening? Brilliant, no?"

"But what do I *do*, sir, once I burst out?"

"Stand there, be admired, be beautiful. Is my gift to you. I leave; for Tommy, no more Count. But you will be most famous boy in town. You will be legend. You do it, no?"

"Couldn't I at least wear underpants?"

"No, no, no. They must see your peaches, your altogether. Is your glory."

"Sir, I'll have to think about it."

"All those men looking at you, not fun?"

He knew me too well. I'd always thought of myself as a tasty morsel men would like to nibble and devour.

""Sir, let me talk to Neil. He advises me."

"Blondie? All right, talk to Blondie. But tell no one else – no one. Must be surprise. If you do not do it, you break my heart. I leave very sad anyway; must I leave with broken heart as well? No, Tommy, you are not cruel, you are kind. You will do it."

Already he had me feeling guilty, if I refused.

"BURST OUT OF A cake stark naked?" said Neil. "Well, that's original."

"Should I do it?"

"Do you want to?"

"Sort of."

He smiled. "Then do it. A randy idea, don't you think? All those men staring at you and slobbering their chops. You'll have more clients than you ever dreamed of."

"You aren't jealous, are you?"

"Hell no. I've got an invitation. I'll be there to look and to cheer."

"Just don't tell anyone."

"I won't."

So I agreed to do it.

THE INVITATIONS CAUSED QUITE a stir. Getting one, Mr. Neddy was radiant with joy.

"Invited to a party at my age! How deliciously exciting! Because of you, dear Peaches. Bless your sky eyes fringed with lashes, your sweet full lips, your frisky peter, your luscious plump behind! I shall be there in my finest togs. And so will everyone. Nibblies galore and lots of bubbly. I can hardly wait!"

ON THE NIGHT OF the party Anton accompanied me to the Albemarle, a quiet, elegant hotel that didn't attract the bustling crowds of the Fifth Avenue. He led me through the lobby to a large ground-floor hall with a long table spread with an immaculate cloth rather like an altar, with silverware and neatly stacked plates – obviously, the place where the cake would be presented. From an adjoining room came sounds of partying; the guests were feasting, talking, singing: to judge by the noise, a merry bunch indeed. In a small side room I undressed. Anton led me back to the table. As prearranged, I kneeled on top of it.

"That's it, sir, head down," said Anton.

Summoned by him, several waiters brought the cake in sections and, without batting an eyelash at my nakedness, assembled it around me, tier by tier. It was a marvel of construction reinforced by a hidden framework of cardboard, each piece balanced by the others.

"Good luck, sir," whispered Anton.

As the last pieces were placed carefully on top, shrouding me in darkness, I heard the Count's voice in the next room announcing, "And now, friends, we go to room with monumental cake, marvelous creation, most delicious, most exquisite, feast for eye and palate." The timing was perfect; he had promised me I wouldn't have to kneel there long.

Hidden inside the cake, I couldn't see, but they had left several tiny holes so I could breathe and hear. I detected footsteps all around me, murmurs, ahs of admiration at the cake, then the Count's voice: "This cake, dear friends, is my farewell gift to you. Is gift from heart. Is food, is beauty; take. Let this be golden moment."

"Golden moment" was the signal. I sprang to my feet and thrust out my arms to either side, easily shattering the structure of the cake, and stood there for all to see. There were gasps of surprise, a stunned silence, and then, as it registered that a naked boy was standing there before them, cheers and a mounting ovation.

So far, so good. But I was covered with icing and bits of cake: a sticky, pasty goo that clogged my hair, eyes, nose, and ears, and stuck in patches all over my body, including my buns and privates, right down to my toes. I stood there a sugary mess, barely able to see, not sure what to do next. On an impulse I flung my arms out high in the air, in what I hoped was a gesture of triumph. It worked: the mounting applause was accompanied by cheers, whistles, shouts, stomping feet. A chant of "Tommy, Tommy, Tommy…!" began.

Suddenly several of the guests rushed over to the table and began licking my feet. It tickled; at first I liked it. Then more rushed over, clambered up on the table, and began licking my calves and knees. Still more came; there was a tussle, a fight to get near me, with shrieks and shouts and giggles. When they started on my buns and thighs, it began to look like an orgy. *What the hell*, I thought, *I want out of here!* Then the table tipped over, sending me, the gobblers, and the ruins of the cake crashing on the floor in a jumble.

The Count came rushing over, followed by two burly waiters.

"No, no, no! No taste, please – just look! Do not gobble Tommy, gobble cake!"

Even in that jumble of bodies on the floor, they were licking me. Gently but firmly, the waiters pulled the gluttons off; deprived of me, they started devouring the cake in handfuls, disdaining forks and plates. Others rushed up to join them, while those in the back of the hall, unable to see, were pressing forward to learn the cause of the commotion. It was total confusion.

"Come, dear boy, come!" said the Count, helping me to my feet. "Such cannibals! Such boors! Who would think?"

He hustled me off to the side room, sent Anton for towels, shut the door.

"I am so sorry, Tommy, so sorry. You are not hurt, no? This was not meant. Pigs! Clean off icing, get dressed, get out of here. Otherwise they eat you alive."

I was dazed. Anton brought towels, some moist, some dry, and started cleaning me up, while the Count went back to the party, hoping to restore some semblance of order.

"We'll have you clean in no time, sir," Anton assured me. "Such barbarians!" He wiped me gently, with diligence.

As soon as the worst of the sugary mess was off of me, I got dressed, and Anton and I sneaked out. All around the toppled table the crowd was still gobbling the remnants of the cake, some of them genteelly with plates and forks, but as we left, the chant of "Tommy, Tommy, Tommy…!" started up again.

Back in the Count's suite I showered to get the last of that sugary mess off of me, then fell exhausted into bed and slept. Hours later, in the middle of the night, the Count tumbled into bed beside me. "Poor Tommy…so sorry…poor Tommy…" he murmured, then kissed me on the cheek and fell asleep.

WHEN I GOT UP the next morning, the Count was still sleeping. I dressed, had a hasty breakfast, and left, for I had promised Mother that I would be back in time to go with her to church. I would see the Count again that evening for our last good-byes.

"Thank heaven you're back," said Mother. "You look peaked. They're working you too hard."

"I'll be all right, Mother. I'll catch up on my sleep next week. Let's go to church."

"My dearest, every day of my life I give thanks to the Bountiful Giver for having such a dutiful son. I have no daughter. You are the stay of my declining years."

She'd been proclaiming her declining years for a decade.

At church I knelt at appropriate intervals on the needlepoint cushion in the pew, raised my voice feebly in singing hallelujahs to the Lord of Hosts, and heard the Reverend Blythe proclaim in his sermon, with rather marked conviction, "Oh dearly beloved, in the byways and labyrinths of life things are not what they seem!" Amen.

When, as usual, the reverend greeted us in the entrance at the end of the service, he gripped my hand a few seconds longer than usual and probed me with his eyes. Did he know about the cake fiasco? Had he been there himself last night? His look aside, nothing betrayed him. Our game continued.

At dinner Mother raved about the hymns and the sermon, and Stewart ran on at length about Black Friday on Wall Street. Chained to his desk, he had seen less than I had, but talking about it made him feel important. On all subjects I kept mum.

Later I saw Neil in his room.

"Cake boy!" he exclaimed with a grin. "That's what they're calling you all over town. Also Sugar Buns, Orgy Boy, and Sweets. And the Frosting Kid and Candy. You're the talk of the town. What an orgy!"

"It wasn't an orgy, just a fiasco."

"I was standing in back, couldn't see. What happened?"

I told him.

"Well, like it or not, you've become a living legend. Among the musical, that is."

"I *don't* like it."

"It's even in the late editions of the papers. Listen to the *Herald*." He picked up a paper, read.

" 'We regret to report a riotous event last night in a banquet hall at the Albemarle, that most respectable of hostelries, where a horde of frenzied guests fell upon a monumental cake and devoured it in what can only be described as an act of orgiastic gluttony.' "

"At least they don't mention me."

"And the *Sun*, in a column entitled 'Sunbeams': 'In a musical gathering last night at the Albemarle, a winsome nymph in the altogether burst out of a pyramided cake to the deafening applause of the spectators, whose appetite for icing proved insatiable. In select circles, the young charmer will have a brilliant future.' "

"Oh God…But at least they're being tongue in cheek."

"The *Times*, of course, says nothing. As for the *Tribune*: 'We shall not deign to chronicle certain events said to have transpired in a rented hall at a respectable hotel in this city, lest we seem to be countenancing that most horrid and detestable crime, among Christians not to be named.' "

"Thanks. Just what I needed to hear."

"Look, you're not mentioned by name. And this will bring you scads of clients. Now I *am* a bit jealous."

"I don't need clients, what I need is a vacation."

"Cheer up, Sugar Buns. This will all blow over."

LATE THAT AFTERNOON I saw the Count for the last time. We had our usual four-poster romp before dinner, dined in the hotel dining room, then came back to his suite. There was no question of further partying; Anton was packing already, and we were both played out.

"I leave tomorrow, Peaches. Do not come to dock; I could not bear it. Here, this is for you."

He handed me a small black satin box labeled "Tiffany's."

"Do not open now; open later."

"Thank you, Count. Thank you for everything."

"It is I who thank you; you give me joy. I want to take you with me to Europe, but I must not; I know myself too well. I go to Paris now, lovely Paris. New city, new boy. I would drop you – not fair; I cannot help. We part here, is better."

"Will you come back someday, sir?"

"Maybe, maybe not. If I do, I am changed, you are changed: different. All we have is now – rich and beautiful now. We have had fun, no?"

"We have had fun, yes."

"I shall miss you, little Peaches."

"I shall miss you, too, Count."

He kissed me; we both cried.

"Good-byes," he said. "Always good-byes – I hate!"

With that, he broke away, disappeared into his bedroom, and shut the door. Anton saw me out. "Good-bye, sir."

"Look after him, Anton. Good-bye."

Back home in my room that night, I opened the little black satin box. In it were a pair of coral studs, very flash. I wept.

12

"DEAR CAKE BOY, DEAR Sweets, you're the hottest thing in town. I've had a torrent of requests for your services. I'm doubling your rates as of now: forty for a rendezvous, sixty for an evening, and one hundred for an overnight of bliss. Say the word, and I'll book you for a solid month."

"Please don't. I need a few days off. That cake business got me down."

"Understandable, dear Peaches. It was just a small rowdy element that caused all the trouble. I had only two glasses of bubbly and ate my cake like a gentleman. It was sinfully good, by the way."

"That whole week wore me out."

"Yes, the Count does go at a pace."

"But I miss him. I'm pretty much down in the dumps."

"Yes, take a little time off. This is Monday; see me Friday at eleven. Playing hard to get will only whet their steam. And here now are your week's earnings: one hundred forty dollars, as agreed, plus a bonus of forty from the Count. Save at least some of it for a tidy old age. You may never again have it so good."

"WELL, WELL," SAID MOTHER at lunch. "So we're riding in fancy carriages now, aren't we?"

"What do you mean?"

"Mrs. Flanders saw you on the Avenue getting into a carriage with a liveried coachman."

Mrs. Flanders lived at the end of the block: a Dame of Charity and a busybody.

"Oh that, yes – a client. I had a message for him. He had me ride with him while he read it and wrote an answer. Then I delivered the answer."

"They have you delivering messages to carriages in the street?"

"Sometimes. He's a very special client, a count."

"A count? Oh my!"

"He gives good tips. He sailed for Europe today."

"My son has met a count. Whoever would have thought?"

I had squelched her doubts. Thank God Stewart was at work.

Since I was rolling in money, I gave Mother ten dollars for the week toward expenses, twice what Stewart gave her. She was delighted, but when Stewart learned of it that evening, he turned red, said nothing, glared.

"Watch out," said Neil, when I told him. "That's too much. When she reflects on it, she'll ask more questions."

"My mother has never reflected in her life."

"Then Stewart will. Watch out."

So we worked it out: I'd tell them that this week's earnings included a special bonus not to be repeated.

"And put some of that money in the bank," Neil urged.

"I don't know how."

"I'll show you. I'll take you to my bank."

So I opened a bank account. It made me feel important.

THE NEXT DAY AUNT Jessie arrived, ill announced as always, sporting garnet earrings and a parasol with a carved ivory handle that she brandished like a weapon.

I hauled her luggage up the stoop.

"Come here, both of you," she ordered Mother and me, as she marched into the parlor with a package. "Susanna, this is for you."

From its wrappings she delivered a bronze statuette of a handsome naked youth; I knew him at once.

"This thing has been around my place far too long; I'm cleaning out clutter. A copy of a copy, but a nice piece even so. Where shall we put it?"

Her sharp eye scanned the parlor, lit on a small stand in a corner bearing the bronze figure of a young woman, eyes down, hooded and abundantly clothed.

"There! On that stand! That frumpy Chastity can go."

"But I like it, Jessie," protested Mother. "A wedding gift. It's been in our parlor for years."

"Some wedding gift! The place for it now is in the attic."

Jessie snatched away the girl in bronze, planted the youth on the stand.

"Yes, that's perfect!" she declared. "Thomas, why are you smiling?"

Ganymede replacing Chastity in our parlor! I could hardly wait to tell Neil.

"I like it, Aunt Jessie. Our parlor needs a classical touch."

"But what is it?" asked Mother.

"Ganymede," I announced. "In Greek myth, the cupbearer of the gods."

"So you know about Ganymede?" said Jessie.

"Oh yes. Dr. Murdock mentioned him at school."

"Hmm…I trust he didn't mention too much. Thomas, you're positively smirking."

"I like it there, Aunt Jessie. You have good taste."

"So you're basking in aesthetic satisfaction. That's new. How does a messenger boy learn about art?"

"By keeping my eyes open. I'm in and out of homes all the time. I see people's parlors. They have nice things; I like them."

"In that case you shall come visit me and see what's in *my* parlor. Taste, like manners, must be nurtured. I shall help form yours."

"I'd love to come, Aunt Jessie."

This was the first time Jessie had ever invited any of us to visit her.

AT DINNER THAT EVENING Stewart spouted on about Black Friday. Mother and I had heard the story twice already, but Jessie hung on every word.

"Then finally gold hit one fifty-five!"

"One sixty!" I blurted out.

"All right, one sixty," said Stewart. "How did you know, cream-puff?"

"I read it in the papers, big bug."

"There were thousands milling about in the streets," Stewart continued. "Men were weeping and screaming."

"Really!" said Jessie, impressed.

"And every time the price went up," I interposed, "the crowd gave a deafening roar. You could hear it for blocks."

Stewart scowled; Jessie gave me a penetrating look.

"Thomas," she said, "I think you were there."

"Well, I was. I was delivering messages for one of our clients, a count."

"Why Tom, you didn't tell us," said Mother.

"I was so busy last week, I guess I clean forgot."

"You have a count as a client?" Stewart asked.

"All last week. He's gone now; he sailed back to Europe."

"Isn't that exciting!" said Mother. "Thomas has met a count."

"Funny you didn't mention it earlier," said Stewart. "There's something fishy about this."

I gave him a good, hard look. "See here, brother mine, I'll do my job and you do yours. Okay?"

"That's fair enough, Stewart," said Jessie.

"Yes, it is," added Mother. "I don't want my boys squabbling. You both have good jobs and I'm proud of you."

And that, I hoped, was that.

JESSIE LEFT IN THE usual whirl the next morning, to descend on her daughter in Philadelphia. Before Mother, spieling of the Higher Harmony, could change her mind about Ganymede, I hustled Chastity up to the attic and nestled her in a dusty black walnut cradle, beside a child's chamber pot and trunks of rotting lace. Then I moped about.

Later, in an idle moment, my eye fell on Mr. Whitman's *Leaves of Grass*, which the Count had given me but I had had no time to glance at. I glanced now and was astonished to find a celebration of manly and robust love: men kissing, men holding hands. I had had no idea that such love could find expression in print in the modern world, least of all here, in this city, today; I devoured the volume greedily. But in the front, in bold green ink, was an inscription: "To Tommy, with affection, hoping you will richly know manly love of comrades, from your comrade of moment, Count." Reading it, I thought again of the Count and moped about still more.

"Enough of this!" Neil announced on Thursday. "The Count's gone, and that's that. You've rested up; it's time you got out again. We'll hit some new places tonight."

So I put on my fawn nut huggers and the coral studs from Tiffany's, and, feeling flash, went back into the world of night. Neil looked stunning, tall and slim in a dark coat with velvet lapels and matching trousers with a stripe of braid, his blond hair faintly pomaded, his smooth, fine features the epitome of elegance and grace.

First we went to a saloon called the Horseshoe, where patrons gathered around a horseshoe-shaped bar, talking boisterously. It was a mishmash of rough-looking types and tourists, including even a few women, eyeing one another warily; I knew no one, felt uncomfortable. Neil ducked away to chat with a friend, and suddenly, there right in front of me, was Walter Whiting, dressed like a good bourgeois in frock coat and cravat.

"What are *you* doing here?" he demanded.

"What are *you* doing here?"

"Touché."

"Beg pardon?"

"Never mind. Look, given your tender years, this isn't the place for you. A lot of riffraff come here."

"That's why it's such fun."

Neil returned, I introduced them; they nodded, barely spoke.

"Let's cut this place," said Neil. "I don't like it."

"We're taking your advice, sir, we're leaving," I told Whiting.

He nodded; we left.

"That man back there," said Neil, once we were out on the street, "he's interested in you."

"Walter Whiting? Nonsense."

"He is. I can tell."

"How?"

"The way he looked at you. And the way he clammed up, once you introduced us. He's not bad looking, you know. The kind of maturity that some boys go for."

"He's complicated. With you, I know where I stand. With him, I don't."

Neil took me to another saloon called the Mischief, where our entrance provoked shouts of "Cake Boy!" and "Sugar Buns!" Out of the crowd came Metcalf, looking blithe and jovial.

"How's Orgy Boy? I thought I'd done everything, but jumping out of a cake tops them all. Hey, Sugar Buns, I didn't know you worked for Mr. Neddy. You've been holding out on me."

"What's to tell?"

"Plenty! That gala: you were the Count's boy for that whole week!"

"So?"

"I was there at the orgy. But I couldn't get anywhere near you — those rowdies wouldn't let me."

"Sorry about that."

"No matter; I connected with one of the waiters – what a stud! Can't talk now, I'm warming up a guy at the bar."

And he was off.

"Who was that?" asked Neil.

"A chum from school – a bit of a lecher. Hey, let's try the Garden." We left.

As we entered the bar at the Garden, a creature in a garish blond wig with plumes, her face fiercely rouged, and wearing a skirt with bells that jangled, sashayed up to me and tapped me on the shoulder with her fan. It was Lady Cheshire, whom I barely knew.

"Well if it isn't the Frosting Kid himself! Hardly recognized you with your clothes on. I'll have to tell the Duchess of Marlboro. After your *succès fou* at the gala, she didn't think you'd deign to set foot in the Lust Garden again."

She blew me a kiss, scurried off.

Here too there were cries of "Orgy Boy!" and "Sweets!" Then the crowd at the bar started up a chant of "Tommy, Tommy, Tommy!" till the bartender shushed them. It seemed like I'd never put that damned gala behind me. Neil went to get us some beer, and the moment he was gone, there again, looking pertly wise and ironical, was Walter Whiting.

13

"ILL MET BY MOONLIGHT, proud Titania," said Whiting.

"Beg pardon?"

"Like a bad penny, you keep turning up."

"Well, speak for yourself." Suddenly band music erupted in the garden. "Do you dance?"

"At my age, certainly not."

"Oh. I thought we might. Dance, I mean."

"What a grotesque idea!"

"Older men can dance; I've seen them. Some of them are very good dancers."

"Not this one. My appetite for farce has limits."

"Well if you don't dance, Mr. Whiting, why *are* you here?"

"To watch the buzz. It amuses me."

"The 'buzz'?"

"The quirks and follies of the age."

"Oh. Well, I guess I'm a part of that, aren't I?"

"You certainly are."

Neil arrived with two foaming mugs of beer. "Someone bought

these for us – I'm not sure who. It seems you're quite a hit. Hello again, Mr. Whiting."

Whiting nodded.

"Neil, Mr. Whiting is here to see the follies of the age. Let's show him a folly, let's dance. Mr. Whiting will hold our beers, won't you, Mr. Whiting?"

We thrust the mugs at him and darted off to the dance floor; he looked half amused, half perplexed, a mug in either hand. In no time we were hopping about with the best of them, doing a frisky polka, a dance that Neil had taught me at home. Out of the corner of my eye, I saw Whiting on the edge of the dance floor, mugs in hand, watching us.

When the polka ended, I was about to reclaim our mugs, but the band struck up a quadrille, a square dance that Neil had also taught me, and he yanked me back to the dance floor, where dancers were forming up in foursomes. Suddenly Lady Cheshire appeared with the Duchess of Marlboro, whose false red hair was piled up high on her head and sprinkled with glitter, and whose rouged face beamed a garish smile over a bulging bodice and a jangling skirt.

"So this is the famous Sugar Buns!" said the Duchess. "The Duchess is honored to shake her lovely shins with you, you golden, shameless boy!"

"Thank you, your grace."

"Ooh, listen to him – he's charming!"

Within seconds Neil and I were partnering them in the rowdy steps of the dance; they giggled and squealed. At intervals I and the Duchess frisked past Walter Whiting.

"See the fun you're missing?" I shouted over the din of the music.

"You've got a lot to learn!" he shouted back.

"Teach me!"

"Teach you what?"

The pattern of the dance whisked me and the Duchess away, but a minute or two later it propelled us past him again.

"Greek!" I shouted.

He looked startled; we pranced off.

"And *amor socraticus*!" I yelled, when we came near him again.

He said nothing, conspicuously took a sip from my beer.

"What'll *I* get out of it?" he shouted, when we came his way again.

"The unbearable beauty of boys!"

And off we danced.

When the quadrille ended, our partners planted a noisy kiss on our cheeks, squealed, and scurried off. Again, I was about to reclaim our beers, but the band started playing "Jeanie," and Neil held me on the dance floor. Once again the young man in lederhosen, wearing a jaunty cap with a feather, and showing a shapely pair of legs, sang in a rich tenor voice.

I dream of Johnny with the light brown hair,

Borne, like a vapor, on the summer air...

Neil and I hugged each other tight, swaying gently, almost imperceptibly, to the music.

I see him tripping where the bright streams play,

Happy as the daisies that dance on his way...

Neil and I weren't lovers, but in his arms I felt safe. The whole world shrank to this one fragile moment, this perfect unity, as we rocked gently, pressed tight against each other. I hoped Walter Whiting was watching.

When the music stopped, we broke apart, became two again. We looked for Whiting, but he had disappeared, and so had our beers.

Neil smiled. "He's jealous. He thinks that we're lovers."

"YOUR BROTHER CHECKED US out," Mr. Neddy reported, when I saw him on Friday.

"Stewart was here? Good God!"

"Yes, dear Peaches. He asked all kinds of questions; I gave him a real song and dance. Yes, Thomas Vaughan works here; one of our best messengers, in fact: very prompt, very diligent. Yes, he gets overnight postings; that shows the measure of our trust. Yes, he delivered messages recently to a client who's a count. Who exactly are our clients? None of your business, sir; our operations are strictly confidential. Good day, sir, good day. Hee, hee. That took the wind out of his sails. Oh, I squelched his doubts good and proper. He left here feeling just a bit of a fool."

"Oh God, I hope so."

"Not a very nice young man."

"You're telling me? He's been on my tail for years."

"Thank the gods of discretion that I didn't overdo the rouge today. I don't think he'll trouble us again. Now Peaches, I have a client for you, one we can't put off. But first, here are two notes addressed to you, both dropped off today. Since that gala, you've been *so* popular."

The first note was in a neat, round hand: "Dear Thomas, You are a beautiful boy. I'd like to fuck you. -- Smitten." I showed it to Mr. Neddy.

"Sooner or later all the boys get them. From Smitten or Discreet or Dark Lover or Lord Byron or Socrates or whomever. Someone who lacks the means – or courage – to approach you through the service. A nuisance, nothing more." He wadded it up, tossed it on the floor.

The other note was written in a slack, more casual hand: "Dear Thomas, If you are serious about lessons in Greek or whatever, come to my place at three tomorrow. I'll save you an hour. -- Walter Whiting."

This note I didn't show to Mr. Neddy. If I saw Whiting, I'd be off duty. But *would* I see him? I wasn't sure.

"Now Peaches, you have a client for tonight. Someone influential in local politics."

"Like an alderman, you mean?"

"Something of the sort; ask no more. Please do all you can to accommodate him. It's important for the operation."

For the first time, Mr. Neddy seemed slightly nervous.

THE ADDRESS HE SENT me to was a shabby rooming house squeezed in between a liquor grocery and a livery stable on the far East Side: for the Frosting Kid, a bit of a comedown. I asked for Mr. Casey, was directed to a room in back. The door was opened by a short, squat man in his underwear, powerfully built, with a black walrus mustache and lustrous thick black hair. He waved me in, scanned me.

"Oh lad, yes, oh lovely, lovely, lovely, like a fresh sweet whiff of spring. Oh glory, how nature weaves her wiles! The very sight of you has done me a power of good!" He spoke in a rich brogue; his breath smelled of onions and liquor.

Even as he spieled, he was undressing me; no introductions, no small talk. My shoes still on, he tossed me face down on the bed, pulled down my pants and underpants, kissed and pinched my buttocks. His touch was rough.

"Oh iligant, iligant! Peaches indeed, oh iligant!"

Suddenly he pulled my underpants back up, rolled me over, looked me in the eye.

"Oh lad, you're not a Catholic, are you? No loies now; tell me true. Are you a Catholic, yes or no?"

"No, sir."

"Praise be to all the saints in heaven!" He flipped me back over and yanked down my underpants again. "Sure, you're a randy rum slut of a lad, and ripe for reamin'!"

Indeed, he reamed me royally, panting and grunting all the while; the bed springs squeaked. I tried to relax into it, as Neil had taught me, but somehow I just couldn't. Luckily he shot right away, then pulled out of me and lay on the bed.

"Oh iligant, iligant! Oh lad, what a curse and a blessin'! I'm in raptures of joy, I am. I needed it, oh, I needed it bad!"

"Glad to oblige, sir," I whispered, though I hurt.

Suddenly his features darkened. "What have I done? It's ruined I am! What, oh what, have I done?"

Buck naked, he fell to his knees on the floor.

"Holy Mother of God, Mary most merciful, forgive me, forgive me, it was just a moment of folly with a sly little punk of a lad. He's not a Catholic, niver would I do it with a Catholic, oh niver, niver, niver. He's a pagan or a Methodist or somethin', but not a good Catholic, no, nor an Irishman either, sweet Mary, I'd niver do it with one of me own!"

While he ran on like this, I was scrambling into my clothes.

"Merciful Virgin, a thousand times I've prayed to St. Jude, no use, I've still got the itch. I'll confess, I'll see Father Pat tomorrow, he's not a hard one, not him, I'll do seven acts of perfect contrition, I swear I will, sure in no time I'll be back in a state of grace."

For quite a while he wallowed in contrition, his voice rich, fluent, and desperate. Finally, dressed, I was ready to leave. "Excuse me, sir..."

"O Lady most gracious, don't flush me away down the privy hole of hell, to burn with Mahometans and Baptists. That lad, that winsome little punk of a whore, was a lure, a trap, an ambush set in me way by the Divil. Oh he's a cunning one, the Divil, took advantage of a poor simple man like me. Oh it ain't daycent, it ain't daycent at all!"

"Sir..."

"Niver a word of loie will I tell about it. 'Twas the drink that did it, sure, 'twas the drink. Good Irish whiskey, more's the pity. O shame, O degredation!"

I tapped him on the shoulder. "Excuse me, sir, the money..."

"What? Oh Jaysus, the punk wants his pay!"

Still on his knees, he lumbered over to a stand by the bed, opened a drawer, grabbed some greenbacks, and thrust them at me without our eyes ever meeting.

"There! Take your thirty pieces of silver. Divil's brat, be gone! You've brought me foul temptation."

I took the money, tiptoed out. As I closed the door behind me, he invoked "Jaysus Mary Joseph" and launched into a litany of saints.

THE NEXT DAY I saw Neil; I told him the whole story.

"An alderman, you say?"

"Or something like that. Mr. Neddy was pretty vague."

"Probably an alderman or councilman or commissioner. Neddy had no choice; he had to send him someone."

"Why?"

"Those people have connections. Young America exists because of connections. Neddy answers to someone who answers to someone else."

"Neddy doesn't run Young America?"

"Of course not. He's just a paid employee, a flunky."

"Then who does run it?"

"Some kind of ring. Aldermen, judges, whoever. They pay off the roundsmen and the precinct captain, and the higher-ups as well."

"Then it's all about corruption, isn't it?"

"You bet. The whole city's corrupt. If it weren't, Young America wouldn't exist, or the Garden or those other places either, and we couldn't play our little games. Think about that, the next time you hear reformers rant."

"Wow! You've given me a lot to think about. But that alderman, or whatever he was, do you think he'll want me again?"

"Not a chance. His kind never sees the same boy twice. But for

Neddy's sake, I hope you satisfied him."

"I did my best, but it's tough competing with the saints. Funny, isn't it?"

"And sad."

"Yes, funny and sad all at once."

"But once you've had your laugh," said Neil, "mostly it's just sad."

One thing was clear. After the alderman, I was in a mood for Walter Whiting and Greek.

14

WHEN I PULLED THE bell pull of the brownstone on East Eighteenth Street at three p.m. sharp on Saturday, I was going over a list in my mind.

1. Don't correct him.
2. Don't interrupt him.
3. Say "fellatio."
4. Remember that you're here to learn Greek.

With number 4 in mind, I'd decided against nut huggers, wore checked trousers that were sporty and casual.

This time a maid answered the door and showed me to the study in back.

"Good afternoon, Tom. You're punctual; that's good." He was wearing his lounge jacket and a tie that was slightly askew.

"Good afternoon, Mr. Whiting."

"Welcome again to the chaos out of which order sometimes comes. Sit anywhere you please."

The study's rich clutter was bathed in afternoon sunlight. Once again my eye went to the statuette of the naked boy on a stand. He noticed.

"Ah yes, it does get one's attention, doesn't it? Let's have a closer look." We approached it. "Tell me what you see."

"A real charmer with thick, curly hair and a smile. A slender build and nice plump buns."

"Yes, a behind to die for. Anything else?"

"That smile, those half open eyes: he's a sly one. Knows he's being looked at by a man. He feels the man's eyes on his face, his dingus, his bottom."

"He likes that?"

"Does he ever! No babe in the woods, for sure. He's been around."

"A prostitute?"

"Maybe, maybe not. But he's anticipating. He'll let himself be had by the man, but on his own terms, not the man's. He's a little devil, I'll tell you. That man had better watch out."

"Hmm, interesting. I got it on my first trip to Paris, when I was just awakening to all this. Saw it in a shop window, had to have it: a compulsion. I went in, haggled with the woman, got it. It's been in my study ever since."

"If it were in mine, it just might drive me crazy."

"I know. From time to time I put him away, but somehow he always sneaks back."

He went over to a chair and sat in it; I sat on a hassock at his feet.

"So you want to learn Greek?"

"Yes, sir."

"Why?"

"Dr. Murdock said that Greek is the gateway to wisdom. And then, you've mentioned Socratic love. I'd like to know more about that."

"It's all there in Plato: *paiderastia*, the love of boys."

"Could you spell that, sir?"

This time I'd brought pen and paper; he spelled, I wrote.

"So a pederast is not a dirty old man, Tom. He's a lover of boys. I have been, on occasion, a lover of boys. A boy is not a finished thing; he's a promise, a beginning. He needs encouragement and guidance. I want to help him, to be a part of his maturing. That, Tom, is what Socratic love, or Greek love, is all about."

As he spoke, a look came over his face I'd never seen before. His eyes shone; he was transfigured.

"Dr. Murdock never told us anything like that."

"Of course not. Moralists call this kind of love a crime against nature. If so, Socrates and Plato were criminals, Michelangelo and a lot of others, including even, if the truth were known, Lord Byron."

"All of them?"

"All of them."

"Wow! *Paiderastia*: it's a beautiful word."

"It's a beautiful language. Latin marches and clanks; Greek dances."

My eye fell on a print half hidden under a heap of papers on a chair nearby. "What's this, sir?"

"What?"

"This print."

I retrieved it from the heap of papers. It showed a man with a dark beard, seated, facing a standing boy; both were naked except for their cloaks.

"I've never seen a picture like that!"

"Good heavens!" he said, taking it from me. "I've been looking for this for days."

"It was on that chair. But what is it?"

"It shows a painting from a Greek vase."

"Like in Keats's poem, you mean?"

"Exactly."

"But what's happening?"

He smiled and passed it back. "You tell me."

I looked at it again, more closely. "This must be Greek love. The man has reached out and is fondling the boy's testicles. He sure knows what he wants, and he'll get it."

"And the boy?"

"He's new to it, a virgin. He avoids the man's eyes. Modest, shy – the opposite of that statue. But he can't hide his thing – just look at it!"

"Ah yes, his *phallus impudicus*."

"Sir?"

"His wanton cock."

He spelled; I wrote.

"Thank you, sir. I like that: *phallus impudicus*. It sounds so impressive in Latin."

"But to get back to the print…"

"Oh yes. This is the man's first move; they haven't even kissed."

"They haven't?"

"Oh no. But the man's caught him at just the right time; the boy is shy but ready. He wants it, he really does."

"Wants what?"

"The man's spunk, his God-given seed."

"'God-given'?"

"Yes, sir."

"Hmm. I confess I never thought of it like that. Go on."

"The man: what a buck! He just reaches out and grabs him – gently, of course. If the man had kissed him or taken his hand, the boy might have squirmed away. But if a man grabs your balls, you can't; he's got you. That stud knows what he's doing."

He took the print back, scanned it. "I've looked at this print a hundred times, but you're telling me things I'd never noticed."

"But it's all so obvious – to me, at least. Of course I've been approached by lots of men, though never *that* way."

"Hmm. I keep forgetting about your…uh…occupation. How will you ever find time for Greek?"

"I just will. It will stretch my mind a bit."

"You might not like me as a teacher. I'm very demanding."

"So was Dr. Murdock. Demanding teachers are the best."

"You know, Tom, I'm having trouble squaring 'Peaches' with Plato."

"Sir?"

"I have trouble grasping how a young man known as 'Cake Boy' –"

"You've heard about *that*, sir?"

"Heard about it? I *saw* it."

"You were there?"

"Who wasn't?"

"Oh God…!"

"You were quite fetching in the altogether, with that icing all over you."

"You're the last person I wanted to see it. It was all a mistake, a fiasco."

"Be that as it may, Tom, I continue to wonder how a young man known as 'Cake Boy' and 'Honey Buns' –"

"Oh no, sir!"

"What?"

"'Sugar Buns,' not 'Honey Buns.' "

Too late, I caught myself; scratch rules 1 and 2.

He gave me an acid look. "I stand corrected: 'Sugar Buns.' But I'm still wondering how such a young man can take a serious interest in Greek."

"It's an adventure. It will take me places I've never been."

"No doubt. But when I look in your big baby blues, I see dollar signs. You go with men for money."

"Yes, sir."

"So I can't help thinking of all those men you've slept with."

"Oh, we don't do much sleeping."

"Have you ever thought, really thought, about what it is you're doing?"

"Oh yes, sir. I'm providing a service. We all are. The Boys of Charity, or the Society for the Relief of Aged Affluent Males. Some men just want to get it off with a boy; we give them relief. But some are old and lonely, so we make them feel less lonely. What's wrong with that?"

"A lot, if I could just put my finger on it. Are you aware of the risks you're taking?"

"You mean the pox, sir? Neil warned me long ago to avoid anyone with sores or a rash."

"Neil? You mean Blondie, that exquisite?"

"My best friend. He taught me all I know."

"Another thing to hold against him. Tell me, where is your mother while all this is happening?"

"With the Dames of Charity, or reading *Little Women*. She's read it twice."

"You have no other family?"

"My brother. He came sniffing around once, asked a lot of questions, but Mr. Neddy had a lot of answers. That settled him."

"Tom, have you ever thought about your future? Will you even have one?"

"Oh yes, sir. These are my top earning years. I'm putting money in the bank. Neil's bank."

"Him again. You seem to have an answer for everything."

"Yes, sir."

"Must you always agree with me?"

"As you wish, sir. I want to be agreeable."

"And must you always say 'sir'?"

"No, sir. No."

"Enough of this. Where were we?"

"You were going to teach me Greek."

"So it would seem. All right, Greek. We'll start with the alphabet; it's simple enough. Just repeat after me: alpha, beta, gamma, delta…"

"Alpha, beta, gamma, delta…"

"…epsilon…" He made it sound enticingly erotic.

"…Epsilon…"

Our eyes met. He gave an exasperated sigh, then: "Oh hell." He stood up, I stood up. We went over to the ottoman – the ever-present, most necessary ottoman – where he began peeling off my clothes. And there went rule number 4.

Soon we were both naked, he sitting, I standing in front of him, just like the figures in the print. And just like the man in the print, he reached over and fondled my testicles. No one had ever done that before.

He smiled, whispered. "Your little nuts, your little eggs…your marbles, your nuggets…your little pomegranates, your puffballs, your plums…Soft as marshmallows, then hard as rocks…"

I'd never thought of those hairy little bags as beautiful; they just hung there, like it or not. Now, hearing his litany, I knew better. Some of the things he said were kind of funny, but I wasn't laughing. I was in a delicious daze. This man was an enchanter.

Gently he lay me down on the ottoman and pleasured me. He wasn't physically as adept as Neil (who was?), but every movement, every gesture was charged with feeling. He was teaching me passion. Passion isn't frenzy; it's a slow, steady flow of feeling that rises from the depths of you and reaches into the depths of another. Touched by it, nothing is obscene.

Then I pleasured him. When he spent, I waited until we had disengaged and were lying side by side, and then, with his eyes on me, I received him. He wept. Not a word was spoken.

I lay there in his arms for I don't know how long; time had been suspended. Finally he sat up.

"We'd better dress. Your mother will be expecting you, and Botticelli is waiting for me. He's fiercely jealous, demands most of my time."

Getting up, I sank to my knees, pressed my cheek against his thigh, and hugged it with both arms; he ran his fingers through my hair.

"I don't want to go," I said.

"I know."

We got dressed.

"Walter, when can I have another lesson?"

"Lesson?"

"Greek."

"Tom, I can't think about that right now. I can't think about much of anything." He was still teary-eyed.

"Oh. I was hoping…"

"I'll send you a note through Neddy."

"Soon?"

"Whenever."

We kissed; I left. We hadn't even gone through the alphabet.

15

FOR DAYS AFTER THAT, in bed at night I fondled my testicles, while whispering, "My little pomegranates, my puffballs, my nuggets…" Having fallen in love with every other part of me, now at last, thanks to Walter Whiting and the Greeks, I'd got around to these. But I also thought about Walter himself, his talk of *paiderastia*, his gentleness, his feeling; I thought about him a lot.

Neil knew that something was up, wormed it out of me; in the end I told him everything.

"I had a hunch this would happen. Don't tell Neddy. You're not supposed to see clients on your own; it cuts into his income."

"I don't think of Walter as a client."

"What does he do for a living?"

"Lectures and writes books. The Italian Renaissance, ancient Greece, that sort of thing."

"Hmm. Why don't I check him out?"

"I'm sure he's on the up-and-up."

"I'll check him out anyway."

Two days later I got Neil's report.

"Walter Whiting is an author and critic of note. He's published a major work on the Florentine Renaissance, articles on Socrates and Plato, and a book of essays on Shakespeare's sonnets and the English Romantic poets. Quite a catch, kid. Not rich but well off. A townhouse here and a home in Hartford; he divides his time between the two. His wife is in Hartford."

"He's got a wife?"

"And a daughter, too. Why are you surprised? Half our clients are married."

"But Whiting preaches *paiderastia*, the love of boys, and does he ever practice it! He's good in bed, I'll tell you."

"Well, he's complicated. That should make him interesting."

I couldn't get over it: this unabashed pederast had a wife! And not one word to me about her. I was dismayed, hurt, jealous, confused; mostly confused.

ALL THAT WEEK I waited for a note from Walter via Mr. Neddy; none came. Instead, I got another note in a neat, round hand:

"Dear Thomas, Why won't you look at me? Why won't you at least acknowledge my existence? I yearn for you, you pitiless, adorable boy. -- Anguished."

I shrugged, threw it away.

"DEAR PEACHES, YOU SAUCY little peter-eater, since that gala you're *so* in demand! Quite on a par with Blondie, Rod, and Cuddles." (Blondie, I knew, was Neil; as for the others, I hadn't a clue.) "But for tonight I have something special for you."

On Mr. Neddy's calendar I could see, scrawled in red, "Peaches: Platonists."

"Yes, the Platonists. They meet monthly, but they're on a budget, can afford our services only once a year. Be nice to the poor things. It's easy; all you have to do is pose. But nothing like that gala; they're gentlemen."

This might be interesting; Walter had mentioned Plato a lot.

AT EIGHT THAT EVENING, squeezed into my sleekest huggers, I approached a large building on lower Broadway where rooms were rented out for banquets and meetings. Posted near the entrance was a sign: PLATONISTS, room 201. I went up, knocked. A key turned in the lock; the door opened cautiously.

"Come in, young man, come in."

Waving me in was an elderly man with pince-nez, his jowly features fringed with gray whiskers, his scant locks crowned with a bald pink pate. As he locked the door behind me, I saw a large empty hall with a podium and rows of chairs. From an adjoining room came the clink of cutlery and the murmur of genteel conversation.

"Good evening, sir."

"Good evening. The members are still dining. Soon they'll come in here for the meeting. I will speak at the podium. And you, Thomas, you will stand on that small raised platform beside it. What we're up to you'll see soon enough. Now if you'll come this way…"

He led me to a small side room, shut the door.

"You will disrobe here. Please hurry. They'll be coming in soon."

I undressed; he watched with titillated glee.

"Oh excellent, excellent! Thomas, you will certainly inspire us. Now please put this on."

He handed me the skimpiest underpants that I had ever seen: a sort of loin cloth, like the rags you see in pictures of savages.

"I'm supposed to put *that* on?"

"Certainly. You can, with effort. It's what models wear, when posing. Male models, that is."

Squinting through the pince-nez, he watched, as I squeezed and wiggled into the damn thing; it wasn't easy. From the lecture hall came sounds of footsteps and talk; the Platonists were assembling.

"Please adjust yourself now. Out there you mustn't squirm or scratch."

I did my best, but my marshmallows weren't too happy.

"I will address the group from the lectern. At a certain point I will call you in. You will stand on the platform; I will help you assume the necessary pose. Speak to no one; no one will speak to you, or even dream of touching you. Nothing untoward will happen. Think of yourself as a model – a statue, even. Please don't get an erection."

Don't worry, I thought. *If they're all like you, I won't.* Everything about him – the jowls and gray whiskers, the pince-nez perched comically on his nose, the stray hairs sprouting from his ears, the pink pate – said fogy and left my doodle limp.

My host – he never introduced himself; I called him the Professor – now went out and joined the gathering. He had left the door slightly ajar, giving me a view only of the lectern; from sounds of talk and the scraping of chairs, I could imagine a group of ten or twelve taking their seats. The Professor went to the lectern, cleared his throat resonantly; the room was quickly hushed.

"Good evening, fellow Platonists. Welcome to the twenty-fifth of our monthly symposia, dedicated as always – though with needful discretion – to the Higher Sodomy. Yes, *higher,* I do insist. As Platonists we acknowledge the baser passions but we scorn them. The soul craves Beauty, strives toward it, seeks to possess it. But to love a beautiful *thing* is to clutch at an illusion; we must love Beauty itself, the Supernal, the Absolute. A beautiful thing – say, a stunningly handsome youth – is but an invitation to a higher Good, a lever to propel us toward lofty aspirations. To launch us on this quest, we have secured the services of a young man whose beauty is striking. We are indeed fortunate to have him with us tonight. In contemplating his beauty, you will of course show the discretion for which the Platonists are known. Thomas, will you please come out."

Of course he caught me readjusting, for the thirteenth time, my nuggets. So I patted them down as best I could, assumed a soulful look, and went out.

As I entered the hall, an audible sigh arose from the members. With a quick glance I took in the scene: a dozen of them of all ages, dressed properly, sitting hunched forward on their chairs, their gaze intently on me. I recognized no one; thank God, Walter Whiting wasn't present. I stood on the low platform, facing them. The Professor came over and whispered.

"Stand up straight, Thomas, with your weight more on one foot than the other, your arms hanging loose at your sides. That's it. Don't be so amiable; please, not a hint of a smile. Look proud, look insolent."

I raised my chin a notch, pursed my lips slightly, stared into the middle distance. "That's it: aloof. Excellent, excellent!"

Sighs of appreciation from the members. The Professor returned to the lectern.

"Dear fellow Platonists, beauty must enhance, uplift us. The young man here is an emanation of the Ineffable, a splinter of the Divine. Contemplating him, we must rise above the immediate and fleshly, glimpse the Absolute. If we meet the challenge, he will be our gateway to Truth."

He went on in this vein for some time. As far as I could tell, I was in turn a thing, an illusion, a lever, an emanation, a splinter, a gateway. Then: "Thomas, you may rest a while."

I stepped down from the platform, sat on a chair behind the lectern. And not a minute too soon. Aloofness and insolence were tiring, and I was stiff from posing. Meanwhile the members were conversing softly, but with animation.

"Not Apollo, certainly."

"No, no, nor the David either."

"Perhaps the Eros of Praxiteles – the one in the Vatican."

"Yes, yes, that divine loveliness, almost ethereal."

"But with a touch of the sensual, don't you think?"

"Decidedly."

"But nothing Michelangelesque."

"Oh no, at the antipodes from that."

I hadn't the slightest idea what they were talking about.

The Professor called me back to the platform, where I reassumed my pose. Twelve pairs of eyes devoured me.

"And now, fellow Platonists, we shall behold beauty in its fullness, in its sheer stark splendor: beauty that sparks the divine madness of Eros, but can vault us to the pinnacle of bliss. Thomas, you may remove the pouch."

Thank God, I thought. *My puffballs are killing me.*

I snatched the thing off and tossed it over my shoulder, a gesture that prompted a chorus of gasps, and murmurs of "Cheeky!" and "Daring!"

"You may approach the model," the Professor announced. "Those who feel inspired may indite an ode or sketch. Otherwise, contemplate. But remember our rule: no one within six feet of the model. That gap is a sacred space."

They crowded round, gazing at me from every angle. With a quick, furtive glance I saw that two had brought out pads and were sketching, while another – a poet, I assumed – was scribbling; the rest of them just stared. I got a general impression of starched collars, neat cravats, drab clothing void of stripes or braid; they would have been at home in my mother's parlor, among the doilies and bric-a-brac. But several were young and good-looking. To control my doodle, I had always resorted to algebra, solving complex equations in my mind. Clearly, I was going to need a lot of it to keep my *phallus* from becoming *impudicus*.

"Ah, the beauty of forms!" the Professor rhapsodized. "The grace and elegance of a face...the slender arms and tapering fingers...the divine, svelte thinness of hips...the perfect rounded contour of a buttock...This, dear friends, dear Platonists, is but the first modest step in our experience of beauty. We must not linger here, we must progress from form to essence, we must bathe ourselves in the dazzling beauty of the Absolute!"

He was bathing in the Absolute; the artists were sketching; the poet was scribbling furiously; the rest were ogling; and I was getting an erection. To curb it, I plunged deep into the binomial theorem.

"The Absolute is the unutterable, the indescribable, the unimaginable: the One, the All, the Supreme, confounding in its glory the petty urgings of bestial desire!"

By now, inching closer, they were decidedly less than six feet away. Some of the geezers were pop-eyed, and though I couldn't see it, I would have sworn that one of them was panting. For the briefest instant my eyes met the gaze of one of the artists; young, he winked. Within sight of all, my dingus leaped to attention. A soft chorus of *ah*s. I gloried in it, allowing myself the slyest of smiles.

"Thomas," cried the Professor, "you will retire at once and clothe yourself. The meeting is adjourned!"

As I ducked away to the side room, I heard a babble of talk. The poet was chasing about to retrieve scattered sheets of foolscap from under the soles of the other members, who, heedless of him, were clustered about the artists, extolling or critiquing their sketches. From the lectern, the Professor kept announcing that the meeting was adjourned.

Minutes later, when I had dressed, the Professor joined me in the side room, pouch in hand. I expected a vigorous rebuke, but he seemed crestfallen as he pressed my earnings into my palm.

"I'm afraid, dear boy, that it's not easy aspiring to the Absolute. The baser instincts do take over."

Now that I had my clothes on, most of them didn't notice me leaving, though one looked longingly and another blew a kiss. As the Professor saw me out the door, the poet was beseeching his comrades in tears -- "Stop! Stop! You're treading on my ode!" -- while the comrades appraised the artists' sketches with enthusiasm.

"That divine buttock!"

"That pouting lip!"

"The essence of the ephebe!"

"Beyond Ganymede!"

"Sublime!"

Coming away, I was tempted to laugh, but didn't. I felt sorry for them.

16

THAT AUTUMN MOTHER'S INNER radiance was sorely tested. In town to advocate – daringly – the creation of a ladies' gymnasium, Cora Worthington was struck down and killed on busy Broadway by a wagon carrying a full load of Griesbach's Lager Beer: a cruel irony not lost on her followers, since Miss Worthington had been a tireless champion of temperance.

Mother was overcome. "How long, O Lord, will evil rule the earth?" she lamented, seeing in her idol's demise a near fatal blow to the cause of universal peace. Then, as the first surge of her grief abated, over and over again she exclaimed, "A bright star is gone from the sky!" Whatever our opinion of the Sweet Singer of Hackensack (and would that she had stayed there), Stewart and I were sobered by Mother's grief and feared the worst, since she had mourned our father for years, going out in public only in a dark bonnet trimmed with jet, her face hidden by a thick black veil: a great performance that ended only when Aunt Jessie ordered her to toss off mourning and get on with her life. Fortunately, for Miss Worthington she confined herself to black-bordered handker-chiefs, a black crepe fan, and jet jewels for a month.

The funeral in Hackensack, which Mother was too stricken to attend, drew hundreds of weeping mourners, mostly female, and was well reported. No question: in a man's age this woman, now hailed as New Jersey's most famous female resident, had left her mark. With the cooperation of the metropolitan police, who stopped all traffic for three long minutes, the Dames of Charity laid a wreath on the site of her demise – to my knowledge, the only such gesture to have ever graced the muck of Broadway. Mother still spoke of her own inner radiance and the Higher Harmony, and still served our meat with an abundance of broccoli. Uttered amid the screech of midtown traffic, Miss Worthington's last recorded words -- "I love everybody" – were enshrined in Mother's heart.

ONCE AGAIN I MET Metcalf on the street; he had a hurried look, as if rushing from one revel to another.

"So how's the medical student?" I asked.

"Look, I'm just a freshman in college. History, English, biology – what a load!"

"It doesn't sound like you."

"It isn't! I'll probably flunk out. Too many good-looking men on campus. But God, was it a summer!"

"You were active in many directions?"

"Three clerks, five office boys, an importer, a banker's son, a carpenter, and I've forgotten who else. The best was a baronet's son from England, a real dandy; had a fancy hotel suite. 'Most satisfactory,' he says afterward. 'Most satisfactory; quite.' He had my doodle as often as he wanted. Another time, I met a worker in the Park at dusk; a glorious frig in the gloaming, then we got dressed, said a quick good-bye, and left. When I got home, I found I'd put his damn pants on, and he'd put on mine. He got the better of that deal by far. What a lark!"

And he was off again, a lithe young animal, stalking adventures in

City Hall Park.

Metcalf wasn't a b.b. or a pouf, but he wasn't quite a sturdy either. So for him I invented a fourth category: satyr.

"DEAR THOMAS, IF YOU want another lesson, come tomorrow at three. Be prepared to study. -- Walter Whiting."

At last, the summons! But it was rather peremptory, not really what I'd hoped for.

Once in his study again, and the maid gone, I didn't mince words.

"Walter, I've learned that you're married. Why didn't you tell me?"

"Who told you?"

"A friend."

"Well, as it happens, I am. What of it?"

"That changes everything."

"Why?"

"You talked so eloquently about *paiderastia*, the love of boys. You made it sound so beautiful. And yet you have a wife."

"Are you by any chance jealous?"

"I'm confused. And yes, maybe just a little bit jealous."

"Since when does a boy whore have the right to be jealous?"

That stung. "Since he fell in love."

"I forbid you to use that moony word. What happened between us last time resulted from a momentary impulse, an infatuation that will pass."

"It won't! Not with me it won't!"

"It will. Don't think you have a claim on me; you don't. Do you even know what you're getting into? I doubt it."

"What do you mean?"

"I gave you the sunshine without the shadows, and I blame myself for it. What we did together is sodomy: copulation with the same sex, or oral or anal copulation with the opposite sex, always involving penetration. It's a felony, a crime."

"A crime?"

"Punishable in this state by ten years in prison."

I was dumbfounded. "Why?"

"Ask the Christians. It involves a waste of seed; it doesn't procreate."

"So what? That's crazy!"

"There's a lot else you don't know. You're so taken with Greek love. Did you know that Juvenal, the great Roman satirist, denounced Socratic buggers and men in gauzy dresses and bridal veils with a scorn that reverberates to this day? Did you know that? Did you?"

"No, I didn't."

He was pacing up and down. His voice had taken on a hardness I'd never heard in it before.

"Did you know that Saint Paul denounced men who burned in lust for one another, and said that those who abuse themselves with mankind shall not inherit the kingdom of God? In other words, they are *damned*. Did you know that?"

"No, Walter, I didn't."

"Did you know that in Visigothic Spain the penalty for sodomy was castration? And that under Ferdinand and Isabella convicted sodomites were burned at the stake, and their ashes scattered to the wind?"

"No, I didn't. That's awful."

"And that Edward II of England was murdered by having a red-hot spit rammed up his ass, which was thought fitting punishment for his alleged acts of sodomy?"

"That's terrible. Why are you telling me this?"

"Did you know that sodomy was punishable by death in England until only eight years ago? And that in that very same year a man in Dutchess County was sentenced to ten years in prison because – I'm

quoting exactly – 'he did feloniously, diabolically, and against the order
of nature commit and perpetrate the detestable and abominable crime
of buggery against the peace of the People of the State of New York, and
their dignity'? He's doing ten years of hard labor, and many people don't
think that's enough! Did you know that?"

"No." By now I was almost in tears. "Walter, why are you telling
me this?"

"So you'll know the world you're living in. Here in this city, where
the police are paid off, anything goes – until the next wave of reformers.
But that's not how it is elsewhere. So what do you think now of passion
between males, and the glorious love of boys?"

Now I was really in tears. "I don't know...you've confused me...
but...well, it's beautiful!"

He sighed wearily and sank into a chair. "Yes, it is – or can be –
beautiful. But that's not how everyone sees it. I know. I've been wres-
tling with this for years."

A silence. I was perched on the hassock, watching him. He looked
to be in a deep blue funk.

"Walter, do you want me to leave?"

"No." He stirred, sat up. "Enough of this. If you really came for a
lesson, let's get into it."

"I'd like that."

"But I don't know how solid your Latin is. Without Latin, forget
about Greek."

"I can recite Horace's ode about the aging courtesan."

"Not a bad one for a boy prostitute to learn. There's a lesson there."

I started in. After the first stanza he said, "All right, all right," but I
kept on going clear through to the end.

"Your Latin would seem to be adequate. But Greek is harder. Latin
has one subjunctive; Greek has two. Latin has two voices; Greek has

three. You'll have to cope with the complexities of future more vivid and less vivid clauses, and an additional horror called the aorist. Are you up to it?"

"Yes!" He wasn't going to scare me off.

"You'll have less time to go out dancing with Blondie, or to cavort with those preposterous creatures flaunting their fake hair and glitter, and you certainly won't be bursting out of cakes stark naked."

"All right."

"In fact, I wonder if you'll be able to keep up with your professional commitments. They tell me you're quite in demand."

"I'll arrange things with Mr. Neddy."

"You'd better. A scholar's life can be quite ascetic. A bit of a change, don't you think? So let's start right now with the alphabet. I assure you, this time we'll get beyond epsilon."

"Oh, I can do that; I've studied it."

I recited the complete Greek alphabet, then wrote out all twenty-four letters, both small ones and capitals.

"Hmm. How did you learn it?"

"I found a book in our library at home. I studied it yesterday."

"Very well, I'll give you this." He retrieved a book from a shelf, blew a cloud of dust from it. "This is Richardson's *First Year Greek*. Ancient as it is, for the next six months, it will be your lover."

I took it; it looked thick, musty, and drab. "Fine."

"Do the first two lessons. Write out all the exercises. I'll see you at three on Wednesday."

"Fine."

"And don't wear these – what do you call them? – nut huggers."

I had, of course, worn them. "Do they distract you?"

"They are not appropriate. These lessons are not a pretext for fornication. You're really going to learn Greek. I shall be an exacting teacher."

"Fine."

He dismissed me; I took the book and left. I was still reeling from all he had said – his wife, sodomy, those awful punishments; I was totally confused.

OF COURSE I CONSULTED Neil.

"He was different this time – cold, even cruel. Everything he said was harsh."

"He's testing you."

"Why?"

"To see if you'll stick. Do you really want to learn Greek, or is that just a way of seeing him? Is it Greek you want, or him?"

"Well…both."

"Then you'll have to play by his rules. You'll have to sweat it out."

"All those things about sodomy – are they true?"

"I don't know. Probably."

"That's awful! I had no idea."

"He wants to wise you up; that's good. He's stuck on you, I'm sure of it."

"How can you tell?"

"He didn't cancel the lessons, now did he?"

"No. But how will I ever get through to him? He's become a task-master, a tyrant."

Neil smiled. "You'll find a way."

One thing now was certain. This little catamite, this whore, was damn well going to learn Greek. Let Whiting do his worst; he was in for some surprises.

17

SO BEGAN A VERY strange period in my life, when my mind and body went back and forth between study with Walter on the one hand, and my gentle brand of whoredom on the other. It was a tug-of-war between the day that I was reconciled to, because of Walter and Greek, and the night of pleasure and adventure that absorbed me.

In my first lesson we plunged into the present tense of the verb "to be." "Achilles is brave. Socrates is wise. The Greeks are strong. I am short. You are tall. We are rich." Soon we added negatives, then interrogatives, then other verbs as well.

Getting bored with this, I teased some additional vocabulary out of Walter and began adding sentences of my own to the written exercises he assigned me: "The boy is beautiful. Pederasts are handsome. Isn't love divine?" He corrected them straight-faced, without comment.

But I noticed in the well-thumbed margins of the grammar book he had given me some faint penciled entries from another day: "Eros… Frank…Wednesday…" Were these the vestiges of some amour of his youth?

"YOU'RE NOT IN THIS for money, are you, kid? Of course not. You need attention, don't you? And I can give you plenty. You're attracted to me, aren't you? Just a little bit, at least. I'm not so old; not young, but not really old. You need adventure, fun; older men can give you that. And I like to help young fellows along; I'm not stingy. But it's not about money, is it? It's not about money at all."

I'd heard this a dozen times before, so I just let him talk. He was old, wrinkled, pudgy. But the client is always right; the client is a god. And when he started undressing me, I backed away a little, stripped to the waist, so he could have the fun of the chase without too much exertion; I wanted to arouse and satisfy him, not provoke a heart attack. It worked, and I got my forty dollars. It's not about money – not much!

AS WE GOT INTO declensions and conjugations, it was heavy going. Well, I told myself, the way to a man's heart is through his paradigms. I looked for ways to spark up the lessons. Since he'd banned the nut huggers, I wore sporty trousers – checks and stripes, and solid bold colors with a flashy stripe of braid down the side: anything to get his attention. And always an open collar. Sooner or later in the course of the lesson, his eye would go to that patch of bare skin at the base of my neck, so suggestive. The Count had taught me that one, God bless him.

Strict at first, by the third lesson he loosened up a bit. "You did quite well today, Tom. Your exercises show great application."

"Thank you, Walter. Don't I get a reward?"

"Like what?"

"A kiss. Or if you prefer, a pinch."

"No, you do not."

"It's not fair. I'm beating my brains out on this stuff. When I do well, I should be rewarded."

We argued a bit, then finally agreed that for superior performance a reward was appropriate, its exact nature unspecified.

"Fine! So where's my reward?"

"Here!"

He pinched my bottom hard; I yelped. Laughing, he shoved me out the door.

THERE WERE SO MANY, through the autumn and winter, that in my mind their faces quickly faded. Some of them I was glad to forget. The one who only wanted to show me dirty pictures. The one who whispered obscenities through the whole act of love, which didn't exactly excite me. The one who sang romantic songs to me in a cracked voice. The one who talked baby talk. The judge who ordered me to ignore and disdain him; while I looked into the distance and conjugated Greek verbs in a resonant voice, he nibbled my toes, then pulled my whole foot into his slurping, gaping mouth, and shot.

Girls can fake, boys can't; you're either hard or limp. Through all these adventures and misadventures, how did I keep the doodle up? By focusing not on them but on me; not on what they were specifically up to, but on their desire for my body. If all else failed, I closed my eyes and thought of Walter. Usually it worked; he would have been scandalized to know the strange encounters I involved him in. Often I went into a sort of trance, my mind far removed from my body, uninvolved in its acts. And somehow, deep inside me, I preserved a secret place where no one could enter; as long as that was intact, I couldn't feel used or jaded.

TO GET EVEN WITH Walter for that pinch (my bottom had a red mark for days), I wore my nut huggers to the next lesson.

"How dare you wear those things? I expressly forbade it!"

"Sorry. I forgot."

"If you wear them again, I'll slam the door in your face."

"Would you like me to take them off?"

"No! This is a Greek lesson, not an orgy."

For the rest of the session he grounded me in the imperfect tense with ruthless concentration. Then, the lesson over, he surprised me.

"Look at this print of Botticelli's Venus, Tom, just look at it! It gives no hint of the colors, but the draftsmanship is there, the exquisite lines of her face and figure."

He showed me a picture of a naked young woman with flowing hair, floating on a large seashell with a god of winds blowing her to shore, where an attendant waited with a billowing robe.

"Well," I said, "she's a girl. How can I be interested?"

"Don't dismiss her because of that. I can't imagine my life without this Venus; I'd be impoverished, incomplete. Rubens and Titian painted Venus as an ample, voluptuous woman whose masses of flesh could envelop, even smother you. But Botticelli's Venus is an adolescent girl, slender, wistful, virginal, with just a hint of the morbid."

"Morbid?"

"Born of the sea, already she knows that she's going to die."

"Aren't goddesses immortal?"

"Yes, but he paints her as a human. Consummately beautiful, but perishable. Like boys."

I looked a long time in silence and began to see what he meant. To my astonishment, her face haunted me for days.

THE ATTRACTIVE MAN IN his forties who lay down naked beside me and asked only that I touch him gently. As I stroked him with the tips of my fingers, barely grazing his skin, he shut his eyes, panted softly, sighed, and came. I envied his refinement, his sensitivity. Later we both bathed with his almond-scented soap.

Men like him I admired: well-dressed older men who looked clean and fit, smelling of menthol and musk, and who exuded power, wealth, success. I liked to think of my father, who had died when I was seven, as having been just such a man. Was this a way to get close to him, to bring him back to life? Was that what I wanted from these older men, from Walter? I thought of my father as having been handsome, wise, and kind, a keen mind in a beautiful body.

As Christmas approached, Walter decamped to Hartford and his family. At the onset of the holidays, Stewart surprised me.   .

"Tom, let's respect the spirit of the season. If I've been hard on you at times in the past, I'm sorry. From now on, let's not fight."

"Okay."

He gave me a rather decent shirt; I gave him a tasseled walking stick that would plant him in the ranks of the fashionable. My gift to Mother was a volume of vaporous poetry by Serena Witherspoon, the Nightingale of Gotham, which I hoped might dilute the influence of Mother's late mentor and idol, Cora Worthington, and free us from a regimen of broccoli; it didn't.

Determined carnivore though he was, Stewart, in a rather touching gesture, gave Mother Miss Worthington's *Collected Poesies*, 413 pages plus a steel engraving of the author, its gilt pages bound in watered white silk. Mother devoured it, and in an idle moment I too had a glance. The first section, "Tiny Coffins," lamented the deaths of infants, while "Fragile Blossoms" mourned the demise of maidens, and "The Poor Unfortunates" grieved for the lowly. Any corpse was fair game for her Muse. How this massive mortality squared with the Higher Harmony, I couldn't imagine.

By New Year's I had a cold, couldn't go out to make calls. While I sat huddled in my room, coughing and wheezing in misery, I could hear the babble from our parlor downstairs and sniff its potent incense, as

Mother received her gentlemen callers.

I HAD EXTRACTED FROM Walter the promise that, if I did without errors all the exercises for a tricky new tense called the aorist, he would reward me with a spanking.

I studied feverishly, did the exercises without a single mistake. At the end of the lesson I plunked down on his lap.

"I want my spanking!"

He looked surprised; probably he'd forgotten his promise.

"You little devil!" He flipped me over and spanked me. "There! Had enough?"

"No! That doesn't even count. To be spanked properly, a boy's buns must be bare!"

"You punk! You little whore!"

He dragged me to the ottoman, pulled down my pants and underpants, and paddled me again.

"Take that! And that! And that!" He was laughing.

I wiggled, squealed, and, wanting more, begged him to stop.

"And now, to top things off..."

He pushed me onto the ottoman and sank his teeth into my bottom. I came.

"Bitch! Not on my ottoman!"

He ran off, returned with a moist towel, and tried to clean it off. I lay there, dazed.

"What'll my wife think, if she comes to visit me?"

"I'm sorry, Walter. You got me so excited."

"This is my office! Professors visit me here – eminent authors, scholars!" He was dabbing furiously. "Theories of history are studied here, and great ideas discussed!" He was dead serious.

"I couldn't help it, Walter. You're such a man. I didn't mean to interfere with history. I'm sorry, I really, really am."

Sure; sorry as hell.

ANOTHER QUIET ONE: ABOUT fifty, silver-haired, clean-shaven with thick sideburns, neatly dressed in gray broadcloth, dignified, with a deep, calm, pensive voice.

"I ask very little, Tom: just to glory in the beauty of your youth. Lie beside me naked on the bed; let me feast my eyes."

He kissed me almost chastely, then lay down fully clothed beside me, our bodies barely touching, and looked at me with quiet desire.

"In my youth, Tom, I had many lovers. There were times of fervor and ecstasy, rages, torments, jealousies, angry partings and rapturous reunions. I'm past that now, and glad. Every month or two this is all I want, and I pay for it; it's simpler."

After an hour of this tranquil intimacy, he got up, smoothed his broadcloth, kissed me, and had me dress.

"Good-bye, Tom. Thank you for your patience and understanding."

He paid me and saw me out.

He had taught me calm and wisdom, albeit tinged with resignation. I would gladly have seen him again, but of course I didn't; he would need a different fresh face, a different young body. A true gentleman; I missed him.

ON EASTER MORNING I was of course going to church with Mother. The choir would be resonantly joyous, the incense intoxicating, and the Reverend Blythe resplendent in his vestments of shining white silk stitched with gold. Since Mother would be dressed in the peak of fashion, with a new bonnet that she had wheedled out of Stewart, the keeper of the budget, I wore my best formal frock coat and tie, and added a touch of pomade to my hair.

"Well, well," said Stewart at the sight of me, "the little darling is all prettied up for the Easter Bunny."

"Maybe you should pretty up," I replied. "Lately you've been looking rather dowdy."

The truce was over.

WHEN I SAW WALTER next, conspicuous on his desk in the study was a photograph of himself holding on his lap a little girl with lovely long hair who peered at the camera with big, bold eyes; Walter looked every bit the doting father. He advised me that he would be going again to his family in Hartford; the lessons would be briefly interrupted. Was this his revenge for the spanking?

At this point I showed him my copy of Mr. Whitman's *Leaves of Grass*, which I had read several times.

"Walter, I think you should read these poems."

He took a quick glance. "Poems by an American poet? Not likely. All they write about is little barefoot boys and Minnehahas."

"Mr. Whitman writes about men loving men."

"In this country, today? Inconceivable!"

"Walter, you're so immersed in Greece and the Renaissance, you don't know what's happening on your doorstep. Read these poems!"

He pushed the volume to one side of his desk. "I'll give them ten minutes, if I find the time."

When he returned from Hartford, I asked him if he had read them.

"I'm digesting them. Remarkable!"

With that, he plunged me into further forbidding aspects of Greek.

A week later, when I mentioned Mr. Whitman again, he glowed. "Astonishing! In fact, sublime!"

"Well then, you might thank me for bringing him to your attention."

"You did?"

"Yes. That's my copy you have."

"It is? Oh. Then I *do* thank you, Tom. Though unknown to the general public, this Whitman is extraordinary, unique."

"If you've read the poems, maybe I could have them back."

"Not yet, Tom. I'm still digesting them."

His digestion was lengthy. Try as I did to reclaim *Leaves of Grass*, he always put me off. Finally I went out and bought him a copy of his own, and thus extracted from him my copy, now well thumbed.

"Yes, Tom, I thank you for Whitman, even if he came to you from that pretentious fool of a Count."

I'd forgotten about the inscription, but if he was jealous, so much the better. From then on he began quoting Mr. Whitman to me and recommending his work to colleagues and friends. In time he became quite a champion of the poet, whom he was sure he had discovered on his own, without any help from me or the Count. I didn't try to disabuse him.

One afternoon, having drilled me ruthlessly in a whole series of irregular verbs, he shoved the exercises aside and suddenly brimmed with excitement.

"Tom, I've just finished – or almost finished – that essay on Botticelli. I've got the *idea* of it, the heart, the kernel. When I get a hot new idea like this, I'm obsessed. I wake up in the middle of the night, light a candle, and start writing. I go back to bed, get up again, and write. And so on through the night. By morning I'm as groggy as a lover after too much love."

"Ideas can do that to you?"

"They can! Oh yes, they can!"

Now that he mentioned it, he did look a bit frazzled and worn, but his eyes shone. He went on like this at length. It was obvious that, the moment I left, he would return to the embrace of his hot idea. Neil had told me more than once, "You've fallen in love with the most complicated man on earth!" My competition wasn't his wife; it was Botticelli and Michelangelo and Plato and Socrates and Homer: the whole kit and caboodle of the classics, with the Renaissance thrown in!

18

IN MAY CANE THE summons to Boston: Aunt Jessie would devote one week to my cultural and aesthetic education. When Jessica Regina spoke, one obeyed; my Greek lessons and professional commitments would be briefly suspended.

"So our fair-haired boy is going to Boston," said Stewart.

"Stewart," said Mother, "I'm sure you'll be invited another time."

"I couldn't go now, if she begged me. I'm needed on Wall Street. Big operations are pending."

"Like what?" I asked.

"Never mind. Big operations; millions are at stake."

"Oh my!" said Mother.

Stewart's Wall Street doings – whatever a junior brokerage house clerk might be involved in – were always shrouded in mystery.

"Wear your finest clothes," Mother told me, "and pack several changes. Jessie moves in the very best circles. But remember: your aunt is an infidel. Don't let her ungodliness taint your faith."

It was my first trip out of the city alone. Taking a steamboat across Long Island Sound to Connecticut, I marveled at the wide stretch of water, far vaster than the New York harbor, and at the boat's ornate main saloon. And going by rail via Providence to Boston, I sat up in a carpeted parlor car with sumptuous furnishings lit by gas lamps overhead, staring out the window at the dim passing landscape, as the train screeched and jolted on through the night.

Jessica Ames lived in a handsome Greek revival brick row house on Beacon Hill, across from a small park with arching elms. One glance at the decorative ironwork, the polished brass knocker, and the carved woodwork over the windows and door, told callers that here resided a woman of means and taste. A maid in a frilly cap opened the door, greeted me cordially as Master Thomas, but enjoined me to use the foot scraper on the doorstep, before treading into the carpeted hallway.

Aunt Jessie received me in her sitting room in back, enthroned on a gilt sofa, jeweled lorgnette in hand, and mantled in a black lace shawl.

"Good morning, Thomas. How was the trip? Frightful, I'm sure."

"Oh no, Aunt Jessie. I'm a little tired, but it was quite exciting."

"I forget your youth – everything an adventure. Well, come here and kiss your ancient aunt."

I did, again breathing in a whiff of perfume and the scent of clean linen and lace, while admiring her heavy gold brooch. She waved me to a green brocaded armchair flanked by vases with sprays of pink lilac, then eyed me through her lorgnette.

"Thomas, you still have that knowing look, more marked than ever. What are you up to?"

"I'm learning about life, Aunt Jessie. Mother would like it if I never grew up. But I can't be a nice little boy forever, now can I?"

"Certainly not. Name one thing that you've learned."

"Things are not what they seem."

"Hmm. Not bad, for a beginning. A lesson that your mother never has learned, and never will. My intuition, as always, is sound: you're the interesting one in your family. Your brother talks bigger than he is; I don't know where he's heading. Your mother, God bless her, is a piece of scented fluff. But *you* I can do something with, and I intend to. Nora will show you your room. Lunch at 12:30 sharp. Rest before then, if you wish. This afternoon we shall tour the town by carriage."

With a wave of her gemmed hand, she dismissed me.

The bedroom had a small four-poster, red drapes, flowered wallpaper, a white marble fireplace, and more sprays of pink lilac on the bureau. A window overlooked a garden where a blossoming pear tree was bursting into white, and a fountain splattered into a small pond with lily pads.

At lunch, which was served formally, Jessie announced that, contrary to Philadelphia's pretensions, Boston was the cradle of liberty. "As for paltry New York, during the War for Independence it was a hotbed of Toryism, hosting the elite of the British army with banquets, masquerades, and balls. A most shocking chapter of your history."

This theme she pursued during our afternoon tour by open carriage, while screening herself from the sun with her ivory-handled parasol. She showed me the State Capitol, Faneuil Hall, the Old North Church, the Paul Revere House, and other sites, and, as we returned, the Common, where fruit trees flaunted masses of pink and white. It was hugely impressive, bringing the dry facts of history alive.

The next day she gave me the promised tour of the house. Dominating the front parlor was a Flemish tapestry in bold colors, depicting a tusked boar surrounded by baying hounds and hunters armed with spears. It took up a whole wall; I'd never seen anything like it. She then showed me silver candelabras, bronze figurines, Wedgwood china, Venetian glass, and paintings in thick gilt frames, relating when and where she or her husband had acquired each item, why she liked it, and why it was placed where it was. Every room was a composition, each object contributing to the effect of the whole.

"You see, Thomas, your mother becomes attached to things through sentiment. With her, for all her talk of the House Beautiful, true taste doesn't enter in."

She was right. The furnishings in our brownstone had been assembled casually, even haphazardly, with little thought to the overall impression.

She lingered before a portrait of a frock-coated gentleman of middle years, clean-shaven, dignified, elegant.

"My late husband, dear Edmond. A banker who found wise uses for his money. From him I got a taste for fine things, and ample means to indulge it. This house is a shrine to his memory."

The tour of her house had steeped me in wonder and awe. But in admiring certain paintings and bronzes with a classical motif, I made a comment or two about Greek mythology, and in contemplating a nymph that really left me cold, compared it to Botticelli's Venus.

"Now see here, Thomas, for a rank beginner you're much too aware. You didn't get this by eyeing the parlors of the wealthy. Someone's been coaching you. Who is it?"

"Well...Walter." She had caught me off guard.

"And who is Walter?"

"A friend. He's teaching me Greek. He knows all kinds of things and he's telling me about them. It's fascinating."

"Your mother has never mentioned him."

"I haven't told her. He's older than me, a lot older. She's so conventional. She might not understand."

"Well, I'm *not* conventional and I don't understand either. Who is he and what does he do?"

"He's a critic and author. He writes about Greece and the Renaissance."

"You don't mean Walter Whiting, do you?"

"Yes."

"Good heavens, I've heard him lecture. He's brilliant. I have several of his books. How did you meet him?"

"Through a friend. I'm lucky he's willing to teach me."

"You certainly are. You're a charming young man, but for the life of me I don't grasp how a man of his standing finds the time and inclination to teach Greek to a boy of eighteen. Any young college graduate could do it."

I was getting in deeper and deeper. "Well, he has no son, only a daughter. I guess that explains it."

"Hmm. Yes, it might. My daughters are married and off on their own, and I too have no son. The grandchildren are adorable, but they're tiny tots – too young for me to meddle with. Which is why I brought you here. You *do* seem to attract mentors, don't you?"

"I guess I do."

"I wish I'd been grounded in the classics. Instead they gave me music, drawing, French: frilly things. The French, at least, proved useful."

With that, she changed the subject. I hoped she wouldn't come back to it.

THE FOLLOWING DAY SHE informed me that she must catch up on her correspondence; I was therefore on my own. So I wandered the cobblestoned streets of the Hill, admiring stately brick homes, then strolled on the Common, where I attracted several glances, and one sedate-looking elderly gentleman stared at me till his eyes all but popped from their sockets. Boston wasn't so different after all.

ON SUNDAY MORNING SHE announced at breakfast, "Thomas, it's the

Sabbath. While the pious troop to their altars, the Freethinkers Alliance meets in a hall downtown. Given her mildewed piety, your dear mother will have warned you to beware of infidels, but you have a mind of your own. Come along; it will be interesting."

At the meeting were people of all ages, women as well as men. Addressing them was one Laughton Peabody, a powerfully built man of about fifty, tall, beardless, balding on top, with a mass of unshorn locks tumbling down to his shoulders like a lion's mane. He spoke about something called Darwinism, which I'd never heard of, concluding in sonorous tones: "I assure you, fellow freethinkers, this man's ideas will shatter forever the illusion of a God-centered, God-created universe!"

Loud applause followed, but then he was peppered with questions, which he answered skillfully; these people challenged everything. At the end of the session, when he was ringed with admirers, Jessie propelled me up to him, reintroduced herself, and then presented me.

"I enjoyed the lecture, sir. These ideas are new to me."

When he clasped my hand, I felt a flow of energy such as I had never known before.

"Keep an open mind, young man. These are exciting times. The world is in a ferment."

He then turned to greet other well-wishers, leaving me in something of a daze.

"How did you like it?" Jessie asked, as we rode back to the Hill in her carriage.

"That man is incredible. He's a force, an element."

"Quite so. If you come near him, you have to either flee or follow; there's no middle way. I keep at a distance; I'm too old to play acolyte. But I admire him. He was a fiery abolitionist and now beats the gongs for this Darwin, sowing consternation in the ranks of the godly. Men like him are the movers and shakers of the day. That's why I introduced you. I want you to know they exist."

"He's the most dynamic man I've ever met."

"If he hadn't left the ministry, he'd be one of those towering divines around whom young ladies flock and swoon. Be careful, Thomas. Like many men, you have a passive streak in you. You're susceptible. You're malleable."

How right she was! Already I had imagined myself pleasuring this leonine titan. It would be like swallowing fire, like mating with the sun.

THE MORNING OF MY departure, I said good-bye in the sitting room, thanking her for all she had done for me: lessons in taste; the experience of Laughton Peabody; the gift of a silver tie clasp, once her husband's; carriage rides; my first taste of port. She scrutinized me through her lorgnette.

"Well, Thomas, what is it?"

"What, Aunt Jessie?"

"There's something on your mind. Is it girls?"

"Of course not!" I said a little too quickly.

"Hmm. You have a dark secret. Be warned: I'm a nosy and aggressive old woman. In time I shall sniff it out. And by the way, where did you get those studs? They look expensive."

To impress her, foolishly I had worn the coral studs that the Count had given me. "I bought them. I like nice things."

"Bought them on a messenger's earnings?"

"Well, we got a bonus."

"Hmm. The mystery deepens. We shall discuss this again. You have a train to catch. Kiss me and be off."

I kissed her and left. I had enjoyed the visit, but this woman seemed a bundle of enigmas. Was she my friend or enemy? I couldn't tell.

TWO WEEKS AFTER MY return to New York, the local papers announced a lecture by Laughton Peabody on "Darwinism: The Truth about the Theory and the Man." I rushed out at once and bought a ticket, and three nights later squeezed into the packed lecture hall with an excited throng. He spoke eloquently of species and evolution and natural selection and the struggle for survival, none of which I really understood, but he radiated the same force and magnetism that had so captivated me in Boston. Afterward I tried to get near him, but he was pressed on all sides by challengers, journalists, and admirers, including legions of impressionable young females, so I gave it up.

Dreams die hard. Hoping against hope, I alerted Mr. Neddy.

"Yes, dear Peaches, if this Peabody, or anyone answering to your description, requests our services, I shall certainly reserve him for you."

Nursing fantasies of my own fragile flesh being engulfed by the torrent of his energy, I waited three days, four, five: nothing; he was lecturing nightly to a crowded hall. Another two days, three: nothing, and he was gone. Self-deceived, I felt stupid. Whatever the needs of Laughton Peabody, they would be amply met by troops of adoring young women. Not everyone was of the persuasion.

19

"Why, Tom, dear, here's a letter for you."

Surprised, Mother handed it to me at lunch: except for family greetings, the first letter I had ever received in the mail. Recognizing the neat, round hand, I slipped it in my pocket.

"You're not going to open it?"

"Later. I'm hungry." I feigned a great interest in the oysters and the celery soup.

In my room I read it: "Dear Thomas, I am in torment. I love you one minute, I hate you the next. You have robbed me of my peace of mind, my sanity. Be warned: I cannot be responsible for my actions! — Desperate."

Its tone, and the fact it had been delivered to my home address, alarmed me.

I decided to show it to Walter. Seeing him was easier now because, having tipped my hand to Aunt Jessie, I thought it prudent to inform Mother that an older friend was tutoring me in Greek. This in fact pleased her. She thought of scholars as being eminently respectable, and having no knowledge of the classics, revered them and thought them "safe."

"Hmm," said Walter, scanning the note. "There's always a serpent in the garden. You have no idea who wrote it?"

"None at all."

"And he's written you before?"

"Twice. The first was signed 'Smitten,' and the second, 'Anguished.'"

"Smitten, Anguished, Desperate: a clear progression. Maybe a ninny, maybe not. Let me show this to a friend of mine, an amateur graphologist. He analyzes handwriting for a hobby. He might have something interesting to say."

With that, he launched into the imperative. Into the "Go! Come! Fight! Read! Speak!" of my exercises, I had sneaked "Love!" and "Be bold!" Scanning this, he gave me a sharp look and added, pronouncing and writing it, "Know thyself!"

By the end of each lesson I knew now to expect a digression. Though I was still out to tempt him, I had come to realize the risks of tricking him into an escapade that he might later resent. I would do far better to listen quietly and become his confidant.

"You asked once about my wife, Tom," he began. "Lydia is a wonderful woman, a companion and friend, not a lover. She shrinks from the physical as gross; we have an understanding. I married her because I thought my attraction to young men was an aberration I could overcome, and because my father, doctor, and pastor – a triad of worthies -- all urged it. I was drawn to her on every level but one: the passional. Only after our marriage, and the honeymoon fiascoes of my attempts to make love to her, did I grasp what was missing: candescent Eros, the snake of desire."

He was leaning back, slouched in an armchair, while I, as so often, sat on the hassock at his feet. He wasn't looking at me, but at some distant vista in his mind, seemingly unaware of my presence. I listened in silence, knowing that any word or gesture from me might halt the flow of his thoughts.

"Yet long before marrying her I had known the love of boys. My first love was Alex, the gardener's son. I had just turned eighteen. Having graduated from the academy, I was to leave for college in the fall, and came home for the summer, home being a small town upstate. Alex was fifteen, a simple boy, quite charming: tousled brown hair turning at the tips to dusky gold, big brown eyes fringed with heavy lashes, smooth skin, a delicate body that moved with grace. Not what you might expect in a gardener's son; more likely a choirboy, a scholar. His father worked on all the estates in the neighborhood, came to our place just out of town twice a week, and often brought Alex with him to help. I would see them smoothing the graveled terrace of our patio, trimming bushes, raking lawns. His face haunted me.

"Finally I worked up the nerve to speak to him, got a ready response, the beginnings of a friendship. His father was willing to spare him on occasion, if his employer's son wanted a companion, so we took long walks. Slowly, without a single gesture between us, a single overt declaration, our hearts joined. What we talked about I can't even recall; it hardly mattered: we came alive in each other's presence, lived then more intensely.

"Our favorite spot was a hilltop overlooking the Hudson. From it we saw sloops passing below on the river, ferrymen with passengers, tugs towing masses of canal barges lashed together, and racing, smoke-belching steamboats. When the breeze was right, often we inhaled the intoxicating aroma of fresh peaches and plums being freighted to the city. There, all alone, we touched timidly, gazed into each other's eyes, and – just once – kissed. Two innocents groping toward love."

He paused, smiling faintly, lost in memory.

"Of course it couldn't last. My mother saw no harm in it, my father did. An eighteen-year-old, a lawyer's son, spending so much time with a fifteen-year-old, a gardener's son: unseemly. That was just the word he used: unseemly. He told me people would talk; the friendship must cease. I pleaded, to no avail; he insisted. Foolishly, I agreed. After that I saw Alex less, and in the fall I went away to college, found new friends, new interests. I got one letter from him, charmingly misspelled, begging me to write. He was head over heels; I hadn't realized. With my father's strictures in mind, I didn't. When I went home at Christmas, he was nowhere about. The following summer he and his family were gone, I don't know where; I never saw him again. To this day I am haunted by the memory of his charm, his innocence, his simplicity; he revealed to me my capacity for love. Our one kiss gave me a joy that has never been equaled. *Unseemly*: that hateful word…"

For a moment his fist clenched, his features tightened. Then he seemed to wake up.

"Why am I telling you this?"

"It's a beautiful story."

"I find it depressing."

Quickly he assigned me another lesson in the grammar book and propelled me out the door.

"DEAR PEACHES, THIS ONE may be a bit strange. Follow the hints; you can handle it."

The address Mr. Neddy sent me to was a palatial mansion on the upper Fifth Avenue, a freestanding house set back from the street, its tall windows dark, with an imposing stoop mounting to a double front door. In the window of the door was a sign: COME IN. I pushed the door; it yielded; I entered. All was dark inside except for a tall, thin candle in an ornate silver candlestick on a table in the hallway, and another farther on, at the foot of the stairs. Silence; there was no one about. The candles had been recently lit – for me, I assumed. The place was well looked after: no dust, no clutter, everything perfectly arranged.

I advanced down the dimly lit hallway over a thick carpet that muffled my steps, past portraits in heavy gilt frames, and a niche harboring a marble goddess, half draped, with a knowing smile. Attached to the banister at the foot of the stairs was another sign with an arrow pointing up. What was this: hide-and-seek? A treasure hunt? A trap? There was mystery here. Was there danger?

I went up the stairs toward another candle on a stand at the top, in another ornate silver holder. One of the steps creaked, informing anyone within earshot of my passage. Across the hall at the top stood a towering grandfather clock, ticking softly as its glass-enclosed pendulum swung relentlessly back and forth. As I walked past it, it struck eight o'clock. Halfway down the hall was yet another stand with a candle, guiding me to a thick closed door. On the door was a small sign marked with an X. I knocked; no answer. I pushed the door gently; it yielded; I went in.

I found myself in a sumptuous bedroom lit by flickering candles, with a canopied four-poster bed, bureaus with mirrors, a monumental wardrobe, and a fireplace with orange embers and silver ash; a heady scent hung in the air. On a red velvet chair near the door a drowsing gray cat, curled in a perfect oval, looked up at me with yellow slit eyes, purred, went back to drowsing. Only after I had taken all this in did I see the old man in a nightshirt and nightcap sitting on the edge of the bed, looking directly at me.

"Here I am, sir," I announced, standing near the door.

He continued to stare, said nothing.

Something told me to drop the "sir." "Here I am!" I repeated defiantly, then took a step forward; he flinched.

Still not a word. By now I'd become quite adept at reading my clients' wishes. Some wanted just what they said; some wanted the exact opposite; some gave only vague hints. What did this one want?

I met his stare in silence, then stripped off my jacket and dropped it to the carpeted floor. He watched in mute fascination. I took another step toward him; he winced. Was there terror in his eyes?

"I forbid you to look at me!" I commanded. The strength of my voice surprised me. "I forbid it, do you hear?"

He continued to stare. This was really a job for a sturdy, not a b.b., but something drove me on. I took another step, stripped off my shirt and undershirt, dropped them to the floor. His eyes were fixed on my flesh, now bare to the waist.

"You have unnatural desires. You nurse foul and illicit lusts!"

Was this really me speaking? I took two steps closer; he quaked. Now I could see him better: a creased face, bags under the eyes, a quavering jaw; flesh hung in folds from his chin. On one finger, a red-gemmed ring.

"Your mind is diseased; you offend. For this, you will be punished."

Now he was visibly shaking all over. I took another two steps toward him, spoke softly.

"If you touch me, if for even one instant you touch me, I shall punish you. I shall beat you, do you hear?"

His eyes were fixed on my flesh. Under his nightshirt I discerned his erection.

I advanced again, to within easy reach of him, and whispered.

"If you touch my nipple, you will know pain. If you even barely graze it with one finger, I shall strip you naked and beat you. I shall flog your buttocks. I shall lash your swollen prick!"

Now, his excitement was intense. Hand quavering, he reached a finger toward me, drew it back, paused, reached again, grazed my nipple, gasped, and spent.

I stepped back, waited. Breathing heavily, he reclined. I relaxed and listened to the silence, while he stared, dazed, at the ceiling.

"There you are, sir," I at last said softly. "That's better now, isn't it?"

He sighed, nodded.

While he lay there on the bed, free of fear but still in a trance, I retrieved my clothes and dressed in silence. On the chair the yellow-eyed cat stretched, purred, drowsed. When I had finished dressing, I approached him again.

"You're impressive, sir; memorable. Now about my pay..."

Slowly he pointed to a bedside stand: a prayer book, a silver bell, pill bottles, an envelope. I went over and pocketed the envelope.

"Thank you, sir. Quite an experience, unique. You'll be all right now. I'll be going."

I went to the door, looked back. He still lay there, soiled, dazed, jaw quivering, following me with his eyes.

"Good-bye, sir. Glad to be of service."

I left. As I passed the clock in the hall, it struck the half hour. Downstairs I walked soundlessly past the smirking goddess and the somber gilt-framed portraits, and removed the sign that said COME IN from the front-door window, laying it on the carpet. Only when I shut the front door behind me did I get free from this strange, intoxicating dream. I felt drained. By the light of a street lamp I opened the envelope. Expecting forty dollars, I found eighty.

20

"TOM, THE STORY OF my second love is easily told. In college I discovered Greek love in Plato, whom I read in the original, passionately. My professors stressed that Plato used the love of men and boys as a sort of literary ploy, an image; it wasn't to be taken literally. I knew better. From then on, my soul was lodged in Hellas. I adored Greek statuary – the male nudes, of course – and anything that took after it. I even dreamed of those statues: cold yet warm, aloof yet enticingly appealing.

"A year out of college I met a young man at a party who seemed to embody this ideal, a student at a university near the boys' school where I was teaching. Joel had dark languid eyes under bushy black brows, the sharp, clear features of a statue, a chiseled mouth, and white skin like marble kissed by the sun. At one glimpse of him, I yearned to view the naked splendor of his body. He seemed receptive, gave me his address; I sent him poems and rapturous letters, got a warm response.

"When, by arrangement, we met again, he asked me for money. I couldn't believe that the mind in this superb body could so demean itself. Yes, he wanted money, a lot of it; otherwise he would show my poems and letters to the headmaster at my school. I refused; he did.

Summoned by the headmaster, I lied myself blue in the face, insisting that the warmth of my friendship had been misinterpreted; there was nothing untoward between us. The poems and letters were in fact disgustingly gushy but harmless, with nothing suggestive or obscene. The headmaster professed to believe me; I kept my job. But my contract was not renewed. At the end of the school year, I was dismissed."

"That's awful, Walter. I'm so sorry."

"For a long time I was riddled with guilt, wallowed in shame. This continued well after my marriage; it took me years to get over it. Finally, while traveling alone in Europe, I broke out. I had sex with a uniformed Guardsman in London, a *petit Jésus* in Paris, an art student in Munich, a peasant boy in Switzerland, a gondolier in Venice. Oh, I got around at last. Bit by bit, I shed my guilt and shame, the blight of depression, the nagging urge toward suicide. High time, wouldn't you say? High frigging time!"

I listened in silence and awe, amazed at the range and depth of his feelings. Guilt was unknown to me, self-doubt rare, suicide unthinkable.

"What happened to Joel?"

"Who knows, who cares?"

A long silence. Then, as so often, he changed the subject abruptly. "I've heard from my friend the graphologist." He brandished the note, which I'd all but forgotten about. "He says the writer's neatly rounded script is formed very meticulously; it's not his regular handwriting. In other words, he's going to great lengths to disguise it."

"Why?"

"A good question. Is there anyone whose writing you're familiar with who might be sending these notes?"

"No, no one."

"Not even your brother, for instance?"

"No. I'd recognize his handwriting, no matter how he tried to disguise it. It's bold and sloppy."

"Hmm. Then he's disguising it for some other reason."

"What?"

"Maybe he feels shame or guilt – something I know all about. He disguises it even when there's no need. He's irrational. And it was sent to you at home?"

"Yes."

"Who knows your home address?"

"No one except Neil. He would never do this."

"Then the writer has followed you home. He's stalked you. A total stranger, but he's obsessed with you and describes himself as desperate. I don't like it."

"Neither do I. What should I do?"

"Be careful. He may be harmless, but who knows? Don't go out alone at night. Make sure you're not being followed. And let me know if you get another note."

"I will."

"And now for your assignment. An epic undertaking at last: the subjunctive."

He tried to act as if nothing had happened, but from that moment on I felt the cold touch of fear.

WHEN I GOT HOME, Neil called me into his room. "I'm moving out, Tom. I've given your mother notice. I'm leaving at the end of the month."

"Why?"

"I can't receive clients here. I'm tired of rooming houses and shabby hotels. Neddy has found me a suite in a place called – get this! – The Elysium Hotel. It's doable and they don't ask questions."

"I don't want you to leave!"

"I know. But this way I can receive clients in my own place, properly, or if you like, improperly. Neddy will up the fee and we'll split it. It makes sense."

"I'll never see you again!"

"Of course you will. I'll have you over all the time. As soon as I've settled in, I'm going to give a big party. You'll be the first one invited."

"It won't be like having you right next door."

"Things change. We all have to adjust."

So Neil, my friend, my counselor, was moving out. Mother had regrets; I was stricken. Toward the end of the month Mother invited him to a farewell dinner. He came dressed to the nines, talked brilliantly about fashion, the social scene, novels, the latest plays. Mother hung on his every word, I managed a smile, Stewart frowned.

Finally Stewart tried to make an inroad. "I'm doing quite well on the Street. Western rails are hot; anything transcontinental, with 'Pacific' in the name."

"Aren't they risky?" asked Neil.

"Not if you have insider information. I get tips through the firm. I've made a tidy little pile already."

Always the Big Man. It was amusing to see him trying to impress Neil, who remained poised, invincible. But maybe Stewart *was* doing well; he wore a tie clasp that looked to be solid gold.

Neil moved out; Mr. Blake moved in. He was a pudgy accountant who wore wire-rimmed glasses and stodgy square-toed shoes. Gamely, Mother invited him to dinner. He was reticent, dull; the conversation limped. Clearly, a mediocrity. The proof: my brother's Wall Street spiel impressed him. From that time on I consigned him to the limbo of oblivion. After Neil, what a comedown!

ON THE STREET I ran into Metcalf, whom I hadn't seen in months.

"Hi, kid, how are you? I'm in love!"

"C'mon."

"I tell you, I'm in love. He has blue eyes, curly brown hair, the cutest little dick."

"Leopards don't change their spots."

"This one does. I've got religion. I worship the ground his little buns sit on. His kisses are candy; I'm starved!"

"It won't last. With you, it never does."

"It's been three months. For me, that's an eternity. I'm even writing poetry." He produced some sheets of paper from his pocket. "Want to hear it?"

"No."

"Bitch." He stuffed the papers back in his pocket. "I tell you, this is it. When I'm away from him, it's tough. I fall upon the thorns of life, I bleed!"

"That's Shelley."

"Oh. I thought *I* wrote it. No matter, he eats it up. He's a cutie. I can't get enough of him. Calls me 'Pug,' I don't know why. Or 'Cock,' and I *do* know why."

"What do you call him?"

"'Dickey bird' or 'Chick.' His name is Robin."

"Tweet tweet."

"All right, you cynic. Can I help it if I fly to him on the viewless wings of poesy?"

"That's Keats."

"There's just one problem."

"Namely?"

"He's only fourteen."

"You're crazy."

"Crazy with love. My heart aches, and a drowsy numbness pains me..."

"Keats again. You're corrupting a minor."

"He snatched me from the gutter. I'm a changed man, I swear!"

"How do you even get at a fourteen-year-old?"

"I tutor him."

"In what?"

"English, Latin, French, math, whatever."

"You can tutor all those subjects?"

"No, but his parents can't tell. They're hopelessly shoddy. His old man got government contracts, made a lot of money in the war, promoted a railroad, then fell dead. The mother's so busy social climbing, she pays us no mind. He has three sisters but they leave us alone. A lot goes on during those study sessions in his room."

"How did you get the job?"

"An ad in the papers. When I flunked out of school, my old man was furious and ordered me to get a job, so I tried this. The mother wasn't too fussy; she just wanted to dump him on someone. But she's rich, she pays well. You'll meet Robin, if I can get him out of the house. I know: I'll take him to a lecture. *You*'ll be the lecture."

"You're taking a risk – a big one."

"So what? Life is a risk."

"Isn't there something called the age of consent?"

"Who knows? Twelve or thirteen, isn't it? I tell you, I'm in love. If this be error, and upon me proved…"

"That's Shakespeare."

This whole exchange occurred on busy Broadway, with jostling crowds all around us, and shouts and screeches from the traffic. He promised to keep in touch, then wandered off, still raving about his Dickey Bird, his fledgling.

I couldn't get over it: Metcalf, the satyr of yore, in love!

BECAUSE OF AN IMMINENT lecture he was giving, Walter had asked me to come to him early in the morning. The maid showed me in, went to fetch him. While I was waiting in the hall, a woman in her late thirties wearing a lace-trimmed day dress, her dark hair in a chignon with ringlets in the back, approached.

"Good morning. You must be my husband's young man. Tom, isn't it? I am Lydia Whiting."

Smiling, she extended her hand; we shook.

His wife! What did she know? Too much, I was sure. I stammered in confusion.

"Excuse me…I didn't know…I'll leave, of course…Excuse me…"

"Leave? By no means; there's no need. I came down last night from Hartford. Walter didn't tell you? How like him! When he gets involved in his work, he forgets. We're having a late breakfast. Won't you join us?"

"Thank you; I've eaten."

"Then why don't you wait in the sitting room? It's very pleasant there. It gets the morning sun. Ah, here he is."

Walter came rapidly down the stairs, still adjusting his tie.

"I see you two have met. I do apologize, Tom. I quite forgot to tell you of Lydia's arrival. Botticelli, of course: this lecture. We're breakfasting late. If you'll wait in the sitting room, I'll join you there shortly. I do apologize."

In his wife's presence he was genial, urbane; no hint of quirkiness.

"Why don't you breakfast, dear?" said his wife. "I'll show Tom to the sitting room."

She led me to a cheerful room bathed in morning sunlight and settled me on a seat in a big bay window.

"There: I'm sure you'll be comfortable. Would you like a magazine or a book? But of course you have your Greek."

"Thank you; I'll be fine."

"It won't be long; Walter doesn't linger over breakfast. Tom, we must get to know each other. I'll postpone my departure by a day. Walter is giving his lecture this afternoon; I shan't attend. Why don't you come to tea at four?"

Her grace and cordiality amazed me. Didn't she know who I was?

"I'd be glad to, if it's not too much trouble."

"No trouble at all. I'll see you then at four. No need to mention it to Walter. Not now, at least."

"As you wish, ma'am."

"Fine. Good-bye for now. I'll send Walter to you as soon as I can."

Having enlisted my complicity, she left. I looked around the room: vases with flowers, needlepoint cushions, a birdcage with a warbling canary; no clutter, no bronze male nudes.

Fifteen minutes later, Walter came.

"Again, Tom, I do apologize. I should have rescheduled the lesson again."

"We can put it off, if you're busy."

"Maybe we should. Once this lecture is out of the way, I'll have more leisure. Come on Saturday at three. We'll get to the subjunctive yet."

I agreed and left.

I was glad to avoid the lesson, for I could never have concentrated; meeting his wife had totally thrown me. What did Lydia Whiting want from me? She was the soul of grace, but in her I also sensed strength and maybe cunning. If we were going to tangle over her husband, it would be the fight of fights. I was ready. I was more than ready.

21

WHEN I TOLD MOTHER that my tutor's wife had invited me to tea, she was doubly reassured; I hoped she might mention it to Stewart.

She received me in the parlor, another room where I had never set foot, amid plush and brocade and green damask, her blue velvet dress glistening in the lamplight and adorned with a small gold brooch, the whole ensemble in exquisite taste.

"Good afternoon, Tom. How good of you to come."

"Good afternoon, Mrs. Whiting."

"Oh, please call me Lydia. I think of you already as family."

We sat with a low table between us that held a shining silver tea service and a platter laden with goodies. She poured.

"As you know, I live in Hartford with our daughter, who is twelve; she is the center of my world. Walter's work keeps him here much of the time, but he often joins us, especially on holidays. I come here on occasion, usually to shop. Meeting you by chance this morning, I thought – please have some ginger nuts and scones – I thought this would be the perfect chance for us to get acquainted. I always like to know his young men, once the friendship seems firm and stable. I hope my candor doesn't embarrass you."

I looked into my steaming cup of tea. "Well, I guess I'm adjusting."

"Walter and I have an understanding. I too had to adjust at first, since I was horribly naïve and, like most women, knew nothing about such things. A minister's daughter, I was raised very strictly – far too strictly, of course. Walter has helped me get past that; he has freed me. Over the years, in fact, he has shown me more consideration than my father, a tyrant of a man, ever showed my mother, and for that I am eternally grateful. In time he explained – oh, with the greatest delicacy – about his friendships with young men, and I began to understand. It's a part of who he is and, under the right circumstances, brings out the very best in him. Do you follow me, Tom?"

"I think so, ma'am."

"Not ma'am – Lydia."

"Lydia."

"When he's involved in one of these friendships, Walter is transformed. They satisfy some deep need in him. I've learned to welcome them, as long as the young man is serious and presentable. Walter has mentioned you often. When we met this morning, I knew at once that you were just such a young man. I was greatly relieved. And here we are."

"I appreciate your interest and concern, Lydia, but I must tell you that Walter and I aren't so advanced."

"Oh? From the way he speaks of you, I thought your friendship was a settled thing."

"It isn't. He teaches me Greek and other things, but we've really been close only once. He holds back. He's difficult."

"Ah, I begin to understand. If I've presumed too much, forgive me. Yes, Walter can be difficult. He has his quirks and foibles."

"When I see him, I never know what to expect. Sometimes he's warm and open, sometimes he's stern and aloof – even cruel."

"How well I know. Be patient with him; I'm sure he wants you for a friend. But he's had some bad experiences; they've marked him. He hesitates; he's afraid of being hurt yet again."

"I don't want to hurt him. I don't want that at all."

"I believe you, Tom."

"Thank you, Lydia."

She gave me a penetrating look. "Tom, I truly hope that you and Walter will have a long, rich friendship, the longer and richer the better. But there's one thing you must understand. I could never give him up; he's the most interesting and considerate man that I have ever known. There is a part of him that you can never have; that is mine. Just as there is a part of him that I can never have; that is yours."

"I *do* understand. But there are parts of him that we can share, don't you think?"

"What a nice thought! That's what we're doing now."

"I want to be honest with you. Ask me anything."

"I shan't. There are things I needn't know, mustn't know. I know just enough as it is."

Of course: ladies weren't supposed to know everything. The conversation turned to their daughter Janet and their life in Hartford, to Walter's work, to their travels. I couldn't help liking this woman, so gracious, so tactful, so wise. But did I deserve her trust? She knew nothing of what Walter referred to as my "…uh…occupation." If she did, she might recoil in horror.

When I rose to leave, she again shook my hand. "Well, we've had quite a talk, haven't we, Tom?"

"Yes, Lydia, we have."

"We're going to be friends, I'm sure. The world isn't as we are told, now is it? It isn't that way at all. It's full of dark things, strange things, mysteries." From her tone I sensed bafflement, resentment, even bitterness; it faded quickly. "We learn and we adjust."

TRUE TO HIS WORD, Neil, once he had settled into his new quarters, invited a host of friends to a party. I went in striped nut huggers and a boyish waist-length jacket. The Hotel Elysium was a solid brick structure, plain but well scrubbed, on East Sixteenth Street, far removed from the bustle of Broadway and the quiet elegance of the Avenue. When I inquired at the desk downstairs, a sour-faced woman, without looking up from her knitting, directed me to the third floor front.

Laughter and lively conversation could be heard through the door. Neil opened to my knock, dapper and urbane as ever, wearing a coat with a black velvet collar, a yellow silk waistcoat, and a blue cravat, studs and tiepin aglitter, a whiff of pomade from his hair.

"Welcome to Elysium!" he said with a grin. He hugged me and ushered me in.

In the room I found a babbling mass of guests: poufs, b.b.'s, and sturdies, plus assorted others, including an older contingent – Neil's lovers? – who looked on with amusement. Some of the older ones I thought I recognized: guests at the Count's party, a Platonist or two, and other half-forgotten clients. Neil knew everyone.

"Why Sugar Buns, how are you?"

Gowned in mauve satin, Lady Cheshire scurried over to me, her rouged face topped by a towering blond wig, and planted noisy kisses on my cheeks. "Isn't Neil's place simply scrumptious? His taste is divine!"

"The Frosting Kid, no less!"

Now the Duchess of Marlboro approached, her red hair plumed and decked with glitter, her silks rustling, fluttering a black lace fan. She extended a gemmed hand; I kissed it.

"With you here, Orgy Boy, the party's complete, even if you do have your clothes on. Those trousers are absolutely scandalous. Please don't leave too many hearts smitten; the Duchess needs to make some conquests, too."

"I wouldn't dream of it, your grace."

"Dear, dear boy. Well, I must make the rounds: noblesse oblige. I do hope they won't ask for autographs. Have fun. Ta-ta!"

And off she went with Lady Cheshire, gabbing right and left. I couldn't help but wonder what kind of impression – if any -- they'd made on Madame Defarge downstairs.

At a polished oak sideboard Neil poured me a glass of wine. "Your brother has become quite the man about town. I've seen him in a fancy turnout in the Park."

"It must be rented."

"Always with the same young woman. She looks like a tart."

"Really?"

"A fancy one, but a tart."

"Well, well. So that's where all that Wall Street money is going. Keep me informed."

"I will."

Neil went off to attend to his guests, chatting with each cluster of them, refilling glasses, urging them to partake of his goodies. All around me I saw furnishings of velvet and brocade, and fine silver and delicate stemware.

"Peaches, you dear, dear boy!"

Mr. Neddy descended on me, his hair black and glossy, his gray face tinged with rouge, and pecked me on the cheek.

"Blondie is such a dear! When I got an invitation, I wept – yes, *wept!* Tears of gratitude and joy. At my age, to be invited to a party!"

His eye swept quickly around the room and returned to me.

"Neil's little roost is heaven: the glassware, the silver, the doilies!

And all these sweet young faces, these supple warm bodies, these – hee, hee -- luscious little buns! I do like to see young things in action. I shall die, simply *die*, from delight!"

He feasted his eyes on the crowd.

"You're getting glances, dear Peaches, as you always do. Now remember, you're not a freelancer. If you get any – hee, hee – naughty offers, refer the potential client to me."

With that, he was off. Across the room, among the older contingent, I saw – to my amazement – Walter Whiting. He was soberly but elegantly dressed in a frock coat with black silk facings and a dark cravat. I went over to him.

He smiled. "Hail to thee, blithe spirit!"

"Surprise, surprise! You're the last one I expected to see here."

"Botticelli has finally let go of me. Even scholars need a break."

"But you've called our host an 'exquisite.' "

."So he is, but he does it exquisitely well."

I had a hunch that Neil and Walter, whom I had introduced, had come to know each other more than casually. "Well, I hope you're enjoying yourself."

"I intend to. Like Juvenal, I'm a passionate observer of society."

"What are you looking for – horrid vices to denounce?"

"Not at all. I've seen things in Europe: student balls, artists' parties, drag balls. I want to know if New York is catching up."

"Is it?"

"It's beginning to."

Suddenly there was a flurry at the door, as Metcalf entered with his friend. Thin and short, the boy was unbelievably young, with curly hair and the face of an angel; every eye in the room was on him.

"Metcalf's boy," I explained.

Walter peered, then frowned. "A child – a mere child!"

"Well, he's fourteen."

"An infant."

"What about you and Alex? Weren't you and he eighteen and fifteen?"

"At fifteen Alex was more mature; he could make decisions for himself. This boy, I tell you, is an infant. You say they're lovers?"

"Absolutely. Metcalf tutors him. The family of course doesn't know."

"I disapprove. I absolutely disapprove."

"Metcalf says he's in love: totally, impossibly in love."

"No doubt. They always do."

Seeing us, Metcalf brought his Dickey Bird over, introduced him. To my surprise, Metcalf and Walter needed no introduction.

"Good evening, sir," said Robin, on being presented to Walter.

"Good evening, young man. I hope this party doesn't overwhelm you. You're probably not used to such affairs."

"It's my first. Pug thought it might be educational. Of course I can't stay late."

"We're supposed to be at a lecture," Metcalf explained. "What's the topic again, Chick? We've got to get that straight."

"'Ethics in the Modern World,'" said the boy. "We want it to sound dull."

The boy was composed and well-mannered, his pale features framed by a tangle of thick brown curls, his blue eyes clear and bright, his skin satiny, his voice musical and soft: a delicate, fragile doll. A crowd had gathered round; Metcalf beamed.

"So your family lets you go out, supposedly to lectures?" Walter pursued.

"Yes sir, as long as Pug goes with me. For my moral and cultural education. But they really just want to get rid of me. They're Shoddy people, made a lot of money in the war. Nouveaux – what's the phrase,

Pug?"

"Nouveaux riches," said Metcalf.

"That's it: nouveaux riches. They're always going out to parties, and giving parties where they don't know half the guests. It's silly."

"And his pop promotes a railroad," added Metcalf. "At least, he did. He died on New Year's Day."

"I'm sorry to hear that," said Walter. "It must be a terrible loss."

"It shook us up a bit," said the boy. "But I hardly knew him. He gave all his time to that railroad."

"The Something & Pacific," said Metcalf. "He was the vice president."

The boy smiled. "It goes from nowhere to nowhere."

"His ma thinks she's in the social swim," said Metcalf. "But so far, she's only treading water."

"My sisters are just as bad; they're snotty. I'm the youngest, so they don't any of them want me along. They push me off on Pug. Without him, I don't know what I'd do."

"So he's your best friend?" asked Walter.

"Oh yes. He tutors me."

"Latin and math and such?"

"I'm learning lots of things." A mischievous smile. "Most of them aren't in the books."

A ripple of laughter from the crowd. Walter frowned; I smiled.

"You don't feel you're a bit young for all this?" said Walter.

"Oh no, sir. The moment I laid eyes on Pug, I knew that we'd be close. He's so good to me. He's saved my life; I need him. In bed we do everything; it's fun. It all must have been meant to happen. I'm so glad it did."

Walter looked absolutely baffled. I myself was astonished. Had free-living, lecherous Metcalf wrought some kind of miracle? To hear his fledgling tell it, yes.

Others now talked to the boy; he answered with poise and grace. Mr. Neddy hovered on the fringe of the crowd, whispered to me.

"Just look at the two of them! His Dickey Bird – such a little cutie! Do you suppose...? For the operation, he'd be such an attraction; the clients would – hee, hee – positively drool. But no, what am I thinking of? He's found true love. Whom God hath joined together, let no man put asunder. My heart's aflutter. Young love is *so* inspiring!"

Suddenly Neil made an announcement. "Dear friends, I have a little surprise. I thought a bit of music might be in order. And so..."

One of his friends produced a violin and started playing "Jeanie with the Light Brown Hair." Then, while Neil turned down the lamps, the young singer from the Garden appeared as if out of nowhere, in lederhosen and his feathered cap, and rendered in his rich tenor voice:

I dream of Johnny with the light brown hair,

Borne, like a vapor, on the summer air...

Couples formed at once and, embracing closely, started swaying gently to the music: Metcalf with Robin, Lady Cheshire with the Duchess, and countless others. Neil winked at me, crooked his finger, beckoned.

"Excuse me, Walter, I have to dance with Neil. You don't mind, do you?"

"Dance away, Twinkle-toes."

I put my arms around Neil's neck, he clasped my waist, we became a single body moving softly to the music, like so many times before. When I was held by him, everything seemed so simple, so safe.

Many were the wild notes his merry voice would pour,

Many were the blithe birds that warbled them o'er...

Suddenly Neil unclasped me, propelled me over to Walter, pushed me gently against him, and ordered, "Dance!"

Without thinking, I wrapped my arms around Walter's neck, felt his arms around my waist, and breathed in the scent of his linen and cologne, as we swayed softly to the music.

Oh! I dream of Johnny with the light brown hair,

Floating, like a vapor, on the soft summer air…

Finally the two of us just stood there, tightly clasped, oblivious of all around us. The lights came up, the others were applauding us. Surprised, we broke apart; the music had long since stopped. Neil was grinning; I smiled; Walter looked embarrassed.

Another flurry at the door: Metcalf and Robin were leaving.

"Can't stay," said Metcalf. "Lectures don't go on all night."

Robin thanked Neil for the party – "It's been an education" – then waved good-bye to the guests, who waved and blew kisses; they left. The moment the little bird had flown, I sensed the older contingent's gaze fixed again on me. So it goes.

The party went on for hours with dancing, flirting, talking, and a feast of goodies. More than once the Count's name came up; he was reported to be in Amsterdam, Paris, Vienna. I talked to everyone; Walter chatted with a few of the older guests, but for the most part held aloof, watching with a sardonic smile.

He insisted on walking me home. It was a warm summer night with a host of stars in the sky.

"You seem to have charmed my wife. She finds you most presentable."

"I like her, too. She's a lovely person."

"You didn't tell me you'd be seeing her for tea."

"She didn't want me to."

"Hmm. Well, no harm done, since it all turned out so well. She absolutely blesses our friendship."

"Good. I hope that you will, too."

"I consider myself lucky to have her to go home to, even if she's off in Hartford. That crowd back there, what other life do most of them have? I go home to Lydia, my daughter, my work. What does Neddy go home to? A drab flat somewhere, memories, pictures of naked boys. That's not a life, it's the shadow of a life, and that's what awaits them all. Sad, don't you think?"

"Very sad. You have to know when to get out, and have something solid to go to."

"Will you?"

"Of course. I'm not going to be doing this forever."

"So what will you do?"

"I'll tell you that when I see you next, in the bold, bright light of day."

"Hmm. Now you've piqued my curiosity."

"Good."

"Come to me at three on Wednesday."

"All right. But be prepared: I may shock you."

"I'm not so shockable."

"Oh no?"

We were in front of my brownstone; there were people about. I threw my arms around him, kissed him, then hurried up the stoop to the door.

"Damn!" he shouted. "Damn!"

By then I was inside. I shut the door without looking back.

22

ON MONDAY MOTHER RECEIVED a note from Aunt Jessie, who was en route to Philadelphia. Late that afternoon she arrived in a gray velvet bonnet trimmed with frosted grapes.

"I shan't stay long in this city; it's an offense to eye, ear, and nose. Stewart, that tie's askew. Thomas, you're still up to something; we'll deal with that in time. Now both of you, I've decided that I want company, so I'm taking your mother to Saratoga for a two-week stay. We'll sip nasty waters and watch the *crème* of the *crème*, or those who claim to be such. In her absence you will conduct yourselves like proper young gentlemen."

Mother was radiant. "Bless you, Jessie! I haven't been to Saratoga in years. What a sweet surprise! How exciting! But, oh dear, what shall I wear?"

"I shall inspect your wardrobe and advise you."

A flurry of preparations followed; they left late on Tuesday afternoon to catch a night boat to Albany. As soon as the cab had departed, Stewart confronted me in the sitting room.

"You're up to something, all right. I've seen you coming and going.

You don't dress like a messenger: much too froufrou and fancy. You're up to something weird, something you have to hide."

"Like what?"

"I don't know, but I'm going to find out."

"Do you have time for such trivia? You're needed on Wall Street. Those big operations; millions are at stake."

"Maybe something dirty. I'll find out."

"And you're so busy, dear brother, squiring your tart about town."

Instantly his face was warped with rage. He lunged at me; I dodged and fled the room.

"Brat! You'll pay for that!" he shrieked.

By dinnertime he was calmer; we ate in sullen silence. Proper young gentlemen indeed.

ON WEDNESDAY I GOT another note: "Dear Thomas, I am so ashamed. How could I have written you such madness? Forgive those ravings of a starved, lonely man. I am not worthy of you. Of course you despise me. – Contrite."

Reading it, I breathed a deep sigh of relief.

GOING DOWN THE AVENUE to Walter's, I saw a shiny gig drawn by a high-stepping chestnut, heading uptown toward the Park. The folding top was down; in it I saw Stewart, top-hatted, grinning, lightly flicking the reins, and beside him, a young woman in a gaudy bonnet who was giggling and squealing. They didn't see me; I watched as the gig receded in the distance. Neil was right: a tart.

AT WALTER'S, AFTER WE had grappled with the subjunctive, I showed him the note from Contrite.

"So the problem is solved, don't you think?"

"Hmm. Maybe. But his moods come and go pretty fast. Contrite today, maybe anguished or desperate tomorrow. Whatever the mood of the moment, he's still obsessed with you. Be careful."

"I will be."

"Now about these plans of yours that you say will shock me: what are they?"

"I've been thinking a lot. No, I don't want to work for Mr. Neddy forever."

"I'm glad to hear it."

"The novelty is beginning to wear off. I'm tired of being pawed by older men, even the nice ones – and most of them are nice. I have to lie to them, tell them they're attractive, be whatever their fantasies require. I've been called an angel, a devil, a whiff of spring, a glimmer of light, Peaches, Kumquat, Pudding, a tease, a delicious piece, a slut. They want me to be everything except myself. Each time is different, unique, yet it's always the same. I'm tired of it."

"So what do you plan to do?"

"Being kept for a while might be fun."

"You'd really like to be someone's property, under lock and key all the time?"

"That depends on the man. He'd have to be something pretty special. Of course I'd still have to be worrying about my looks – like Neil, who lives in front of the mirror. That might be a bore."

"Have you thought about earning a living?"

"That's what I'm doing now."

"Later, when you're older and can't coast on those boyish looks."

"Oh yes. I'm not afraid of work. Look how I go at Greek. And believe me, that's work."

"And just what might you do?"

"I could be someone's secretary."

"Like whose?"

"Like yours."

"You're joking, of course."

"I told you I might shock you. Your files aren't exactly in order. Do you even have files? I just see piles of papers. You're always losing things, and you fret and fume till you find them. I'd keep your stuff in order."

"Hmm. Lydia has urged me for years to hire someone, but I balk at the idea: don't want a stranger underfoot."

"I wouldn't be a stranger, now would I? And I'd be discreet."

"Paid companion cum secretary: how classic."

"It would mean a lot less income, but I'd make the sacrifice."

"Working for me would be a sacrifice?"

"Of course. You couldn't afford me at my present rates."

"Are you calling me a pauper?"

"Well, compared to some of my clients, your means are, let's say, modest."

"I earn a damn good living! My books sell in select circles, and I'm in demand for lectures all over the place! I explain Greece and the Renaissance to the hoi polloi, and they eat it up. In this country, I *am* Greece and the Renaissance!"

"Well then, maybe you *can* afford me. I charge forty dollars an hour." (No need to tell him Mr. Neddy got half.)

"Forty an hour? Outrageous!"

"Maybe we could work something out. You have a lot besides money to offer. You'd be teaching me Greek and other things. I want to learn all about Socrates and Plato and Greek love, and courtesans then and now, and all the naughty things the Greek gods did, and Botticelli's marvelous Venus, and all the bawdy stuff of the Renaissance. You know all about it. Like your wife, I think you're the most interesting man – not the easiest, God knows, but the most interesting – that I've ever met."

"Don't try to flatter me."

"Why not? I've tried everything else. Once I wanted to be like Neil, but now I want to be like you. Oh Walter, stop being difficult. Your wife has given us her blessing. Haven't I proved myself enough? I've conquered the subjunctive and I'm game for the optative, whatever that is. Can't I squeeze you in between?"

"Are you trying to seduce me?"

I flashed my most winsome smile. "Yes."

"I hadn't planned on this. What'll the maid think?"

"Frig the maid!"

I loosened his tie, pulled it off, and started unbuttoning his jacket.

"Hell!" he said, and began kissing me; after that there was no stopping. Clothes were shed. I draped my pants over the bust of Shakespeare, dropped my underwear on a pile of papers, and dove onto the ottoman with a giggle. But he pulled me up, sat on the ottoman, and had me stand there again in front of him, just like the boy in the print.

"Shhh…" he whispered.

And once again, gazing deep into my eyes, he reached out and cupped my pomegranates: the most beautiful act of possession I'd ever known. Then he stroked my body gently all over, and when I started to say something, put one finger to my lips. We loved in silence; he taught me what touch could do, how there is soul in the fingers. He pleasured me and then, as he again ran his fingers through my hair, I pleasured him and received him; he watched: a holy moment. Then we lay there in each other's arms. It was Eden, it was peace. I wanted nothing else.

Finally we stirred, got dressed. Even then he put his finger to my lips. When I left, he looked at me with wise, kind eyes, deeply grateful. We had said nothing, yet everything. I went home in a trance.

STEWART DIDN'T SHOW UP for dinner; I ate alone. Later he caught me in the hall.

"I want to talk to you!" His voice was hot with rage.

He pulled me into the sitting room, shoved me in a chair, stood over me.

"I had an interesting experience this afternoon. I took a friend to a saloon called the Horseshoe that gets a mixed crowd, including riffraff and poufs. At the bar I heard some of the poufs talking about a boy named Tommy, just the cutest little slut in town: that's exactly how they put it. So I asked one of them, 'Who is this Tommy?' and he said, 'A b.b.' 'What's a b.b.?' I asked, and he said, 'Darling, you must be new. A beautiful boy. He's simply the toast of the town. But he doesn't come here, sweets, you'll find him some evenings at the Garden.' All this in front of my friend, who knows I've got a brother named Tom. So they gave me the address of the Garden."

I started to say something; he yelled, "Shut up!" He went on, still standing over me, red-faced, hot with rage.

"So later, just now, alone, I went to this Garden and asked the thug at the door about a kid named Tommy Vaughan. 'Hey, man,' he said, 'we don't use last names here. Describe him.' I did. 'That sounds like Orgy Boy,' he said, 'the one who jumped out of a cake stark naked. Yeah, he comes here but he's not here now. If you want a piece of that, you'll have to see Neddy at Young America; he's his pimp. And you'd better have deep pockets; he's the priciest screw in town.' "

I started to stand up; he shoved me down.

"Now I get it: the working at night, the fancy clothes, the money. You're a punk, a sodomite! My brother – a known sodomite! What'll my friends think, neighbors, the other clerks at work? You make me feel dirty inside. Holy God, you're a piss-assed whore!"

Now I was angry, too. He'd bullied me all my life; my resentment surged. I jumped up; he couldn't hold me down.

"And a goddam good one, too! Yes, I'm guilty of the horrid and detestable crime among Christians not to be named – buggery! Known in Britain as the Italian vice, in France as German love, and in Germany as the French sickness." (Walter had given me that.) "Because it's everywhere – a conspiracy; you never know who: your worst enemy, your best friend, even *you*. Yes, *you!* Because it may be inherited. Think about *that*, brother mine: maybe it'll surface in *you!*"

"Shut up, you pig!"

"It's a mystery: strange lights have been seen hovering around the erect penises of men on park benches – oh yes, it's been reported!" (Walter had read that somewhere, announced it with a laugh.) "It causes solar eclipses and plagues and famines and invasions – all documented. And earthquakes – the bishop of London himself reported it." (In 1750; Walter.) "But maybe it isn't hereditary after all. It may be caused by shyness, epilepsy, domineering mothers, vile foreign influences, atheism, or enemas; science isn't sure, take your pick. The signs of it are parting your hair in the middle, liking flowers, an open collar, walking too fast or too slow, or carrying a handkerchief." (Some of these were my invention.) "So watch out, brother mine, you carry a handkerchief – I've seen it!"

"I'll knock the spots out of you! I'll beat you to a pulp!"

He came for me; I dodged, and kept a table between us.

"Have you no shame, you little cocksucker? Do you like being known all over town as a punk, a goddam whore?"

"I love it! Your baby brother has been called much worse: pouf, nancy boy, pervert, a juicy little piece…"

"Stop it! For God's sake, shut up!"

"…Mary Ann, queer, degenerate …"

"Shut up, I tell you!"

"…bugger, pansy, pederast…"

He flung a paperweight at me, missed; it crashed against a wall.

"...sodomite, catamite, little Jesus..."

He lunged, caught me. His fist smashed my face, sent me reeling across the room, till I hit a wall and slumped to the floor, lip bleeding.

"...cinaedus, tante, tapette, warmer Bruder..."

The noise had alarmed Margaret and the cook; they stood in the doorway, appalled.

"Oh Master Stewart, Master Thomas," cried Margaret, "for the love of heaven, stop! You'll be doin' each other harm!"

I staggered to my feet, backed away from him.

"But don't worry, dear brother, there are cures: cold baths, mathematics, the brothel, and if none of them works, take the advice of a great Christian philosopher" (Walter again) "and rub your anus with the fur of a hyena – it never fails! Keep that in mind, when you strut around town with your slut!"

"Use that word again, and I'll kill you!"

"If I'm a punk, your girlfriend is a slut. Slut, slut, slut! She's a slut!"

He grabbed a poker from the fireplace and came for me, the anger of years in his eyes. Margaret and Cook screamed. I brushed past a whatnot, it toppled; bric-a-brac shattered. He swung the poker at me; I dodged. Then, as I darted away, he hurled it at me; it missed by inches, clattered on the floor. I ran out the door into the hallway, then out the front door and down the stoop. Coming up the stoop was Mr. Blake, our lodger, who stared at me in astonishment.

As I hurried away down the street, I vowed that never again would I spend a night in the same house with Stewart. We were done; there was no going back.

23

OF COURSE I HEADED for Walter's. It was cooler out now; I hadn't even brought a jacket, had little money on me. At Walter's the windows were dark. I yanked on the bell pull, got no answer, then knocked and knocked on the door, couldn't even raise the maid. What to do? I thought of Neil, but he was bound to be out or, if at home, receiving a client: no time for me to barge in. So I headed for the Garden, hoping to find one or the other there. As I approached the entrance, a man coming out got a glimpse of me.

"Thomas! What happened? You're bleeding!"

He was fortyish with sloping shoulders, thinning hair, a tuft of mustache, and wire-rimmed glasses; I didn't recognize him.

"A fight with my brother. I've got to find Walter."

"I don't know any Walter, but look – you're bleeding all over your shirt. They'll never let you in there."

It was true: my shirt was splattered; I hadn't even noticed. I pressed a handkerchief to my lip. "I've got to find Walter!"

"I'm Doug," he said, extending his hand. "I've seen you at the Garden lots of times, often dancing with that blond guy." We shook. "Hey, it's starting to rain. Tell you what: I live just a spit and a stride from here. Come to my place so I can stop that bleeding, give you some tea, a clean shirt. Then you can look for your Walter."

It was raining, he seemed kind, I was bleeding; I went with him.

His place was more than a spit and a stride from there, which should have tipped me off. We walked and walked toward the East Side past rooming houses and tenements, corner liquor groceries, breweries, a soap and candle manufactory, abandoned carts and wagons, heaps of trash. Assaulted by smells of soap, urine, beer, and manure, I lost all sense of direction, kept dabbing my lip with the handkerchief, which was soon smeared with blood. I was uneasy, but he kept assuring me we were almost there. Finally we stopped before a rather shabby building somewhere over near the river, where he led me up three flights of stairs, unlocked a door, entered, and lit a lamp, then waved me in. A bare room with a bed, a table, chairs, a bureau.

"Not the kind of place you're used to, I'll bet." He closed the door and locked it. "But home is where the heart is, as they say. Sit on the bed; I'll fetch some cotton to stanch that wound."

I sat; he brought the cotton. His hands were knobby, his cuffs worn; he smelled of cheap pomade.

"Don't talk, Thomas, you'll only make it worse."

He dabbed at my lip, then showed me the cotton: a big splotch of red, like a gaudy rose.

"Here," he said, handing me a fresh wad of cotton, "you stanch it, while I start some tea. It's gotten chilly. Tea would hit the spot, don't you think?"

I nodded, took the cotton. He went into another room, put a kettle on, then came back and put cups and saucers on the table. I kept dabbing the cut; the roses were getting smaller.

"Good thing I came along when I did. Otherwise you'd still be wandering the streets in the rain, bleeding all over the place. Who'd have thought? The famous Orgy Boy right here in my modest digs: quite an honor. Your brother cut that lip, did you say?"

I nodded.

"Family fights – those are the worst. Believe me, I know. Hey, there's the kettle."

The kettle was whistling in the kitchen; he went to get it. There was something a bit forced about his patter, but we were strangers and I couldn't talk. He brought the kettle in, filled the cups.

"There! Nothing like a cup of tea, I say, on a night that's wet and chilly. Makes you feel warm, dry, and cozy inside. How's that lip now?"

I showed him the cotton; the roses had shrunk to dots.

"Just about stanched, I'd say. Come have some tea, Thomas. But to be safe, still don't talk. Got to give that lip a rest."

Tea seemed like a good idea; I joined him at the table. The cups were chipped, but who cared? He sipped, I sipped. It was hot and sweet, but tasted slightly odd.

"There! That's better, isn't it? I feel dry already."

I nodded. For several minutes we sipped in silence.

"Just finish up that tea, and I'll give you a nice, clean shirt. Then you can look for your Walter."

I sipped some more: a tinny taste, strange. I felt curiously calm, quiescent, as he rattled on.

"Yes, Tommy boy, I've had my eye on you for a long time, as who hasn't? Just wanted to say hello, share a little chitchat, nothing more. Never got the nerve to do it. You wouldn't have minded, would you… or would you? You're not a snob, I hope? Of course not. Wasn't at that big party where you burst out of a cake naked. Wasn't invited. How do you like that? *Wasn't invited!* Story of my life. But I sure heard – about the party, I mean. You were just the talk of the town: Cake Boy, Sugar

Buns, Candy. That's what I heard all over the place. After that, I knew I'd never get a chance. To say hello, I mean: just hello. Hello, Tommy. Tommy, are you all right?"

The lights seemed brighter now, yet fuzzier; the walls rippled and swayed. His voice sounded hollow and distant, as if echoing in a great open space or a cavern.

"Tommy, I think you need to rest. Here, let me help you to the bed. Stand up...steady now, steady..."

I stood, wobbled; he helped me to the bed.

"There you go now, Tommy...that's it, little Peaches...easy, easy, easy..."

He lay me on the bed. I melted into it, passed out.

How long I lay there I don't know. Dagger points of light danced across the sky of my mind, then streaks of green and orange jabbed and burst and splintered. As a stab of pain entered me, I opened my eyes.

I was lying face down on the bed, my pants and underpants around my ankles, and something was ramming into me, thrust after thrust, each lunge causing another wave of pain. I groaned, then murmured, "No...!" But the thrusts kept on, twisting me in pain, while he panted and gasped. Then as my fists clenched and tears filled my eyes, a deeper thrust ripped my whole body into agony, and I could feel him come. He moaned, sighed, then finally withdrew and lay on his back next to me, naked, breathing heavily. But the pain was deep inside me.

"There, little Peaches...there, you little whore...at last!"

Get out of here! my mind kept telling me. With effort I rolled over, pulled my clothes up, fastened my belt. He was still lying there, panting softly, smelling of pomade and sweat. There was malice in him, venom; what he'd done once he might do again. Slowly I pulled both legs back and then, with a great lunge, kicked him off the bed. Surprised, he grunted, cursed. Before he could get up, I leaped to my feet, ran to the door, unlocked and opened it, ran out. He yelled something behind me, but I ran down the three flights without looking back, and rushed out into the street.

It was chilly and wet; I wove down the sidewalk like a drunk, the pain still festering inside me. Where was I? I didn't know. *Walter,* I kept thinking, *Walter.* My mind must have blanked out off and on, for there are whole stretches of that night I can't remember. I knew that if I just kept heading west, sooner or later I'd come to the Avenue and could follow it north or south, until I came to Eighteenth Street and Walter. But where was west, and would he even be in? I have vague memories of *Lagerbier* signs, beggars, jingling horse cars, lurching drunks.

Finally rain was streaking down my face, as I stumbled up the stoop of Walter's townhouse. Suddenly the door opened, and he came out and started down the stoop, saw me, gaped.

"Tom! You're bleeding! For God's sake, what happened?"

I mumbled something about Stewart and the man; he helped me in and took me to his study, where I collapsed on the ottoman. He fetched a cloth and pressed it to my lip, which was bleeding again.

"Your brother, you say? And some man?"

"The one who wrote those notes. He put something in the tea. I passed out and he reamed me. It hurts, oh God, it hurts! And I can barely walk; I'm wobbly."

"Let me have a look." He pulled my clothes down. You're bleeding there, too. I'll try to stanch it. Then I'm taking you to a friend of mine, a doctor. He may be in; he's just a block away."

Next, I was lying on my stomach on a table in a strange room, naked from the waist down, and heard Walter and another man talking. How I got there I don't know.

"Walter, the only word for this is rape."

"Will the wounds heal?"

"Yes, with time. But there may be other wounds as well; they may take much longer. Young man, are you awake? Can you hear me?"

I nodded.

"I'm going to swab this wound with disinfectant. It will sting, but only for a moment. Ready?"

I nodded. He probed me; it stung, then the pain receded.

"Now I'm going to apply some ointment. This shouldn't sting; it's soothing."

He probed me again; the stuff felt thick and gummy, but it didn't sting.

"There! Now you can dress yourself, Thomas."

While I got dressed, they talked.

"He must rest, Walter. The less he's moved, the better."

"I'll put him up at my place and inform his family."

"If there's any development – persistent bleeding, inflammation, fever – let me know at once."

"How about this drug he was given?"

"That's the rub. We don't know what it was. The effect should wear off in a day or so. Again, if it doesn't, let me know."

"Should we inform the police? That bastard should be prosecuted."

"Hmm. Thomas, can you describe the man?"

"A mustache, fortyish. He smelled of cheap pomade."

"That's half the men in the city," said the doctor. "Do you know where he lives?"

"No. Somewhere on the East Side toward the river."

"Walter, we'd best forget about the police. Probably it's better for the family anyway."

"Agreed. Thanks so much, Ben. I'll see him home."

Then I was in a bed in a strange room at Walter's, and he was at my side.

"There you are, Tom, now rest. I'll be in touch with your family. If you need anything, just ring the bell on this table. I won't be far away. All right?"

I nodded; he left. I slept.

His scum is in me: the words streaked through my brain. A sludge seeped into my body through my rectum. I couldn't see it but I felt it; it was thick and black and sticky, and it stank. Slowly it oozed into every organ, every vessel, every crevice and cranny of my body, mounting relentlessly through my neck into my head and brain. I was paralyzed; I stank.

Walter again: "Are you hungry, Tom?"

I shook my head no.

"Then rest some more. It's going to be all right."

He reached over and, ever so gently, stroked my cheek with his fingers. I shut my eyes and slept. But it wasn't all right. I felt scummy, clogged, dirty; that sludge was still inside me.

24

NEEDLE POINTS OF LIGHT danced and darted. Blobs of green and orange stretched and billowed in the darkness, then shrank to specks and vanished. "We exist to pleasure men," whispered Neil, while my mother lamented, "My boy, my darling, my poor, dear, darling boy!" "Desire is holy," announced the Reverend Blythe, contemplating a glass of ruby wine, while the lawyer, cradling a bust of Cicero, chased me with a fly whisk in his office. "Poor Tom," said Lydia Whiting in a whiff of lilac, "how can such things be?" "Punk! Punk! Punk!" Stewart screamed, then he was sobbing, "I'm sorry, I'm sorry," but I was on a chamber pot and every time I shat, I felt a probing, wrenching pain, and someone wiped me, and I was in bed again and slept. Then Lady Cheshire and the Duchess, wigged and glittery, blew me kisses, till Aunt Jessie cut through crisp and clear: "Thomas, come out of this coma or whatever! I simply won't have it, do you hear? Come out of it at once!" But I was conjugating rare Greek verbs, while the silver-haired gentleman, reclining fully clothed beside me, looked at me with calm, sad eyes. And I woke up.

Blurred lights, walls, a room. Standing by the bed, Walter.

"So there you are," he said. "We've all been worried about you."

I fixed my eyes on him, couldn't untangle my thoughts. That sludge was still inside me.

"Do you want to see your mother?"

"No."

"You should. She's been beside herself with worry."

"No."

"Stewart is distraught. He feels guilty, wants to apologize."

"No."

"And your Aunt Jessie is here, demanding to talk with you."

"No."

"And Neil and Mr. Neddy dropped by."

"No."

"What's wrong, Tom? Hasn't the pain gone?"

"Yes."

"Are you hungry? Shall I get you some food?"

"No."

"You've been through a nightmare. I know it won't be easy to get over it. I want to help in any way I can. Will you let me?"

My voice stuck in my throat; I forced it. "Yes."

"Then try to listen." He sat on the edge of the bed beside me. "Tom, I was put on this earth to love boys, and I've loved a lot of them, sometimes happily, sometimes not. I've learned that it's a boy's need of me that brings out my deepest love. Before, you wanted me – you wanted me a lot – but you didn't need me, not enough. But now you do. You've been broken; you need to be mended, healed. Love, at its best, is a healing. Can you follow me, Tom?"

"Yes."

"Most of the boys I've loved had been wounded. All through their childhood they were pushed and shoved and bullied, and called names like "nancy boy" and "sissy" and worse. They were broken, and with my love I tried to mend them. I can't change the world; it is what it is. But with whatever I have to offer, I'll try to make it up to you. If you'll let me. Will you, Tom? Will you let me?"

Something held me back; I fought it. "Yes."

"If you still want to, Tom, you can be my secretary. You can live here, if you like. You can try to put my papers in order, and it won't be easy. Do you want to?"

"Yes."

"Living with me, you'll have to put up with a lot. I'm cantankerous. I fret and fume. I get angry over trivia: missing studs, lost papers, popped buttons, socks that don't match, scratchy pens. I suffer bouts of melancholia, when everything I've ever accomplished seems absolutely futile, and I'm obsessed by thoughts of suicide. I'm intellectual when I should be sensual, and sensual when I should be intellectual. I'm vain, fussy, arrogant, moody, sardonic, ironical…"

"…kind, intelligent, patient," I whispered, "understanding, perceptive, sensitive, wise…"

He smiled. "You do me too much honor. But I will finish teaching you the basics of Greek and help you to look at things with insight. I'll show you ideas and teach you nuances. I'm inviting you to a Hellas of the mind, more beautiful than any Hellas that ever was or will be. Together we'll read things that will haunt you with their rightness, their meaning, and their beauty. We'll marvel at statuary that glistens in the sun, and at paintings whose lines and colors will amaze you. We may travel together, but even if we don't, just by reading and looking and thinking, we'll go to strange and wonderful places you never dreamed existed. Tom, I think you're crying."

I was.

"Will you come?"

"Yes."

I shut my eyes. A soft beam of light, clean and cleansing, enveloped me, played over the surface of my body. Gathering strength, it entered through my brain and pushed the black, sticky sludge before it, flooding each organ and muscle and fiber with radiance as it drove the ooze ever downward and out through my rectum, till I was clear of it and felt tingly and buoyant and clean. I opened my eyes; he was still there, waiting.

"Thank you, Walter. I feel better."

"I'm glad of it."

"How long have I been here?"

"A week."

"Was Mother here? My mind's been all mixed up. I don't know what's real and what isn't."

"She was here, briefly, and wants to come again."

"And Stewart?"

"Also. He's in tears, wants to apologize."

"And your wife?"

"Also, very briefly. She's back in Hartford now."

"And Aunt Jessie?"

"Was she ever! She *ordered* you out of your coma, but of course it didn't work. A formidable woman. I rather like her, but I think we're going to tangle."

"You are: over me. Did you try to feed me at times?"

"Yes."

"And were you there when I was on that silly pot?"

"Yes."

"Then you've seen me dirty and ugly."

"No, always beautiful. Not quite yourself in your mind, but always beautiful."

"Well, thanks for all you've done."

"Your family all want to see you, and they've a right to. But there's a lot of explaining to be done, and I'm not sure what each of them knows. Where do we begin?"

"With Mother. She's the easiest."

SHE CAME THE NEXT day, first thing in the morning, in fresh ribbons. I had just had breakfast, was sitting up in bed.

"Oh my boy, my dear, dear, darling boy!" She kissed me almost frantically. "Yes, you're better; I can tell at a glance. When I was here before, you didn't even know me – didn't know your very own Mumsey!"

"Not 'Mumsey' – please!"

"Sorry, dear, I forgot you don't like 'Mumsey.' But I prayed to the Bountiful Giver – oh, how I prayed! – and now my prayers are answered. You *are* better, aren't you?"

"Yes, Mother, a lot better."

"You must come home with me at once. This Mr. Whiting has been so wonderfully nice to let you stay here; the doctor didn't want you moved. But now you're coming home to Mumsey – to Mother. Our love, Stewart's and mine – yes, Stewart's, too! – will help you get still better. How could it not? Love is earth's sunshine."

"Actually, Mother, I'd rather stay here. I don't want to live with Stewart."

"Yes, I know you had a dreadful quarrel. Margaret and Cook told me, and Stewart, too. But Stewart has changed. I prayed to the Bountiful Giver that Stewart would mend his ways, and he has. Spiritous liquors may have misled him; he's been cavorting among souls lost to grace. But the Prodigal has returned. He's sorry, oh so sorry! He's in tears – your big brother, in *tears!* He knows he did wrong and wants to apologize."

"Tell him I forgive him. I just don't want to see him."

"You must see him *and* forgive him. It's the Christian thing to do.

So you come right on home!"

"Mother, we've got to talk."

She lowered her voice to a whisper. "Besides, I want to get you away from that man. He's been wonderful, but I don't quite trust him. I think he has designs."

"What do you mean?"

"I'm not sure. But he seems…well…*too* interested in you. A bad influence, I'm sure. You really must come home."

"No, Mother, I'm staying here. I want to. I'm quitting my job with Young America, so I can work for Walter as his secretary. It's all set up."

"Quitting that wonderful job that pays so well? You've been so successful there."

"Too successful. From now on I'm going to be Walter's secretary and companion."

"Companion? He's married, dear; he already *has* a companion."

"He needs another, and it's going to be me. His wife and he have an arrangement. She's met me and approves."

"I don't understand."

"He's in love with me, and I'm in love with him."

"Whatever are you talking about? Boys and men don't love each other. They have friendships, that's all. You mustn't call that love."

"It *is* love. These things *do* happen. They just aren't talked about."

"Tom, I think you're still delusional. The effects of that drug someone gave you haven't worn off. And that awful assault – whatever it was that happened – it's affected your brain. You must come home and rest."

"I'm very clearheaded, Mother. I know exactly what I'm saying."

"I simply don't understand. Men and boys don't fall in love. With each other, I mean. It simply doesn't happen."

"But it does."

"You're not yourself, poor boy. I'm going to consult Stewart. And the Bountiful Giver, of course."

"Yes, Mother, pray for enlightenment."

"And the Reverend Blythe."

"By all means consult the Reverend Blythe."

After further lamentations, she left, vowing to do just that. How easily drama slips into farce.

25

STEWART NEXT. HE CAME that evening, after work. I was glad he'd see me still in bed, with a partly swollen lip; he could use a little more guilt.

"Oh God, Tom, I'm so sorry!" He looked pale, tear-stained, stricken.

"Look, we both said some things we shouldn't have. Let's put it behind us."

"But I hit you, I cut your lip. I threw a thingamabob at you…"

"A paperweight."

"And a poker, too! You're my brother, my only brother, and I drove you out of the house! That's why you got into trouble. It's my fault! I must have been crazy. I'm sorry! I'm sorry!"

"My getting into trouble was mostly a bit of bad luck. And I shouldn't have called your girlfriend what I did. For that, *I* apologize."

"You forgive me then? Say you forgive me!"

"Of course I do. Let's talk no more about it."

"But look at you – your lip is swollen. *I* did it. I feel wretched."

"Your feeling wretched won't help me heal. Now look, here's how things stand. I'm quitting Young America to work for Walter Whiting. I'm going to live with him here. We're lovers, but he's discreet. So there won't be any more scandal."

"I've got to be honest, Tom. I don't understand this business. I don't like it, and I never will."

"You don't have to understand it or like it. You and I don't have to approve of each other or even like each other. From now on, let's just keep out of each other's hair. You live your life, I'll live mine. And the less Mother knows, the better."

"Well…fair enough."

"Has Mother talked to you yet about me and Walter?"

"No."

"She's going to. Just tell her anything that gives her peace of mind."

"Okay."

"And forget about feeling guilty. It doesn't help."

"All right."

"Shake?" I put out my hand.

"Shake!"

We shook on it; he left.

Walter came in later. "So how did it go?"

"He's laying it on pretty thick. The Big Man has become the Guilty Wretch."

"Must you be so cynical?"

"I know Stewart. This mood won't last. If I were living at home again, sooner or later he'd find a way to bully me. He can't help it; it's in his nature. But this should work out fine. I'll be here with you, he'll be there with Mother. He can play head of the house. He's good with the accounts."

"All right, we've squared Stewart. There's still your mother and Jessie."

"Let's worry about them tomorrow."

"Fine. Do you want anything? Maybe some soup?"

"No soup, not now. But for a start, why don't you lock the door, take your clothes off, and get in here with me?"

He did.

MOTHER WAS BACK THE next day.

"Tom, I've talked to the Reverend Blythe and the Bountiful Giver – in that order."

"Already? What did they say?"

"The Reverend Blythe was very reassuring. I saw him in the rectory. I'd never been there before. A perfect jewel of a place – so tasteful!"

"Isn't it?"

A quizzical look. "How do *you* know?"

"The Dames have mentioned it at church."

"Oh."

Awkward slip, good recovery.

"Tom, the Reverend Blythe says that I shouldn't worry. Close friend-ships between men are quite permissible. Our Lord and His disciples, for instance. And David and Jonathan. I asked if there wasn't something about the destruction of Sodom and Gomorrah, but he says that's all a matter of interpretation and not really relevant at all. Then I talked to the Bountiful Giver."

"And He said…?"

"Oh, the same. The words formed in my heart. And now that I've reflected, I realize how foolish I was. After all, the Bountiful Giver has made our bodies in a certain way. Some things are possible and some things are not. I hope I'm not being gross. So when you say that you and Mr. Whiting are in love, you mean a friendship – a wonderfully close friendship – just like David and Jonathan."

"Exactly. He's David, I'm Jonathan."

"I'm sure he's an exceptional person. I feel so much better. This I can understand – almost. I don't want to say what I was thinking, even though I'm not quite sure what it was. It wasn't very nice."

"Did you talk to Stewart?"

"This morning, briefly. When I mentioned David and Jonathan, he said he couldn't agree more. So you and Mr. Whiting have our blessing. Mumsey – I mean Mother – will miss her little boy, but you won't be far away, and I know you'll visit often. And this way things will be easier for both you and Stewart. He's changed, but he might have lapses. So it's all working out for the best."

"And Aunt Jessie?"

"She doesn't seem convinced. You know how perverse she can be. She's coming over this afternoon, says she won't be put off any longer. Try to be tactful. I'm afraid she's in a bit of a huff. I'll be going now, dear. The Dames are visiting the Institution for the Deaf and Dumb."

She kissed me, left. Two down, one to go.

AUNT JESSIE CAME IN gold-embroidered black satin, with her jeweled lorgnette. Though I was eager to get back on my feet, I thought it best to receive her while still in bed. From the outset she peered at me through the lorgnette, its jewels glittering in the sunlight from a window.

"And so, Thomas, your dark secret is out at last, and a vile one it has proven to be. I gather, from the ravings of your addled mother, that you and the famous Mr. Whiting are committing acts of unnatural lewdness together, though your mother seems to think now that you're both as innocent as newborn lambs. Don't expect *me* to swallow *that*!"

"Walter and I are in love. There's nothing lewd or unnatural about it."

"Then you admit that you've lied to your mother – you and Stewart both?"

"We've let her think what gives her peace of mind."

"To *me* you will tell the truth."

"Of course."

"So you and Whiting are – I have trouble even saying it – lovers."

"Yes."

"I know precious little about such things – what lecturers refer to as the 'shameless lusts of Greece.' But they're illicit, immoral, and obscene."

"Only if you're a Christian."

"Don't think that by appealing to my principles of free thought, you'll get off the hook. We freethinkers have a code of ethics, too."

"That's what I'm counting on."

"You're young and impressionable. This man is obviously cunning and manipulative. He's got you under his influence."

"Actually, he's under mine."

"Just what do you expect from this relationship, besides money?"

"Kindness and wisdom. Especially kindness."

"Hmm."

"And I'll learn all about literature and art. As for money, I was doing far better with Young America."

"That's another thing your dear mother seems blissfully unaware of. This messenger work that brought in so much money: it sounds fishy."

"It is. It's really a service that provides young men to older men for money."

"Are you telling me that you're a – it's so inconceivable! – a prostitute?"

"I was, but not anymore. I'm quitting so I can be with Walter. So you see, he's a very good influence."

"My nephew – a prostitute! I'm shocked to the bones!" She dropped her lorgnette; it dangled from a cord secured to her wrist.

"You wanted the truth, Aunt Jessie."

"How could you?"

"Oh, it was fun – at first. I like attention from older men. But then it got to be a bit of a bore."

"You committed immoral acts for them?"

"I was giving them what they needed: pleasure, shame, friendship or the pretense of it, whatever. Many men – especially married, sedate, respectable men – need a bit of wildness in their lives. I helped them to their wilding."

"Just who were these depraved individuals?"

"A hard-working lawyer who wanted me to smash up his office, because at times he hated Law. A pastor who said desire is holy. A fake count who told me that in this whole city I was his only friend. A tired, wise older man – a real gentleman -- who kept his clothes on and asked only to look at a beautiful young body."

"Wasn't it all a bit…well…disgusting?"

"There were a few bad moments, but most of the clients were gentlemen. They were lonely, and I satisfied them. And of course I learned a lot."

"For instance?"

"Everything they couldn't tell their wives."

"You make whoredom sound like higher education."

"It is. Believe me, Aunt Jessie, it is. What I don't know about men!"

"Another matter: your mother says you were assaulted by a stranger."

"Raped."

"Good heavens! It never occurred to me that a male could be violated."

"It can happen, Aunt Jessie. But thanks to Walter – his kindness and understanding – I'm over it. If you ever *do* get over it."

"Hmm. It's the strangest thing, Thomas. When you talk about all this – things that would strike most people as shocking, disgusting, and obscene – you don't seem corrupted or jaded."

"Deep inside me, I've always had a sort of secret room that no one else could enter; part of me is safe there, untouched. That part is still untouched."

Once again, she scanned me through the lorgnette. "You are a remarkable young man. You're quite at my level, Thomas. I shall ponder all this and look for flaws in your thinking. All my life I've taken pleasure in turning things upside down for others; until now, no one has ever done it to me."

"But that's all behind me now. I'm going to live with Walter."

"I shall talk to him. I want to take his measure."

"Fine. He wants to take yours."

"I'm still baffled by all this, and I'm not one to be baffled very often."

"Like free thought, it stretches the mind."

"Hmm. Fetch Mr. Whiting. We're going to have a long, long talk."

I rang the bell for Walter.

IN HIS STUDY THEY were at it for an hour. I rather liked the thought of it: two heavyweights having it out over *me*. Finally Walter reappeared.

"Well?"

"She's a tough old bird – no question. But I didn't give an inch."

"Good. She respects strength."

"So I gather. You seem to have shown her a lot yourself. She admires you."

"So how do things stand, as of now?"

"She's glad you're out of whoredom – she calls it 'those practices' – and coming to live with me. She's decided I'm not a sinister influence. But she's going to keep an eye on both of us."

"What will she tell Mother?"

"That our friendship is intensely intellectual and cultural: a rare opportunity for you. And she wants to meet my wife. We ended up talking about Michelangelo; she rather likes his nudes."

"Then we've squared her."

"For now. But we'll probably have to do it again every six months. She won't let go of you, says she expects you to visit her often. Lessons in taste and such; she wants to shape your mind."

"I know. Are you jealous?"

"No."

"Oh. I wish you were."

"It's time you got out of that bed and got dressed."

"I will. But first, jump in here with me."

"Look, we can't be doing this all the time. I've got another paper to write."

"Frig your paper!"

"Whore!"

"Not any more. I've reformed."

He locked the door.

26

THERE IS A SADNESS in the world of pleasure; I sense it more and more.

Though I no longer work for Mr. Neddy, I drop by the Young America office from time to time, just to keep in touch.

"Why, Peaches, how good to see you! To think that, at my age, a beautiful boy comes calling! You're warmed me to the cockles of my heart. God bless you, dear, dear Peaches!"

He gives me the latest gossip, though never about his clients of the moment: a new bar has opened, a bath has closed; the Count has been reported in Berlin, Monte Carlo, Rome; Amsterdam is quite the place to visit. He doesn't change: always the cheerful flirt, with a hint of that sadness underneath.

I'M WORRIED ABOUT NEIL. When I saw him last at the Elysium, he spent much of the time in front of a mirror, turning this way and that, combing his hair one way and then another.

"No use," he said, "I'm losing it."

"Losing what?"

"That boyish look."

"You still look boyish to me."

"Not like two years ago. It's fading."

"So what? You're still young and good-looking. Lots of men are attracted to you."

"Young and good-looking is fine. But with a boyish look you've got everything. Like you, you little bastard; you've still got years to go."

"You need Greek."

"Oh sure."

"Or Botticelli or something. Don't stay so fixed on looks."

"Looks are all I've got."

"You're crazy."

"I tell you, they're all I've got."

My best friend after Walter, so refined, so intelligent, hard and smooth and glittering as a diamond, but now he's locked in a losing battle with time. Sad.

METCALF IS ALL CUT up; he came to me in tears. He's been fired as a tutor, accused, denounced, forbidden to see his Dickey Bird again, and threatened with arrest. One of the boy's sisters snooped, saw or heard something, tattled to the mother. Sobbing, he begged me to apply for his job as tutor, see the boy regularly, pass messages between them. Feeling sorry for him, I was tempted, but on Walter's advice I declined; I trust Walter's judgment. It dismays me to see Metcalf, with his sinewy body and pantherlike tread – Metcalf, that tireless hunter, that blithe celebrant of Sodom on the Hudson – reduced to a blubbering mess. As for the fledgling, God knows what he's going through, deprived of his only friend. Maybe Metcalf broke a law; I don't know. If so, in the words of Dickens's Mr. Micawber, the law is an ass. For me, desire is holy.

WHAT'S BECOME OF MY clients? Most of them are fading from my mind.

Do they remember me? I doubt it. I was simply one in a long series of charming young men whose services they hired. I'm sure the lawyer is still rampaging in his office with a boy; that the corseted businessman still grudgingly sneaks time away from his ledgers for a romp; that the Platonists are ogling and sketching, and the Irishman sinning and praying; that in Monte Carlo or Rome or Vienna the Count is calling some rented boy his only friend in the city; that once or twice a year the Reverend Blythe invites a young man to savor a glass of ruby-colored wine, before drawing him toward the sweetest of communions; and that the old man in the nightgown still summons a young adventurer to enter his darkened mansion and follow a trail of signs and candles to his room, where he awaits him with terror and desire. What illusions we clutch at, what fantasies we feed!

STEWART AND I SEE each other rarely, by choice: no tensions, no scraps. Neil, who gets around more than I do, glimpses him in restaurants, at the theater, in the Park, always with that cheap-looking girl. He dresses flash, but not in good taste: garish. He's running with a fast crowd that Mother would never approve of, but who am I to judge? A broker now on Wall Street, he's making money hand over fist, spends a lot; some of it, at least, goes to Mother. The Flash Age, they call it: easy money, fun times. Walter says that these things work in cycles; after every boom comes a bust. Back in '57 there was a bad smash; it helped kill our father. What would Stewart do in a bust? Always playing the Big Man, he has no center, he drifts. I'm tougher than he is, though he doesn't know it, or want to know it: sad.

MOTHER STILL GOES TO the Dames and the Aged Indigents, and worships weekly in the marbled grandeur of the Reverend Blythe's Church of Christ and All Angels. I go with her partly out of filial duty, and partly to witness the spectacle, when his gaze meets mine at the door, of the Reverend's invincible composure; I have yet to dent his poise.

Aunt Jessie, Stewart, and I have always dismissed Mother as foolish and trivial, but maybe she's the smart one after all: like Lydia Whiting, she knows what not to know. Truly happy in her illusions, she turns melancholy only at the thought of my father, now gone these many years, and at the prospect of losing her sons. But I drop by fairly often, and so far, Stewart shows no sign of moving out. On a precarious budget she raised us free from want, and aside from the imposition on her sons of broccoli, has never done harm to anyone. Her pleasure comes from good works; I see no sadness there.

IS THERE SADNESS IN Aunt Jessie? One wouldn't think so. "I'm an old woman with edged ideas and a tart tongue," she has told us more than once, "and I have no thought of changing." But her grooming me to shape my taste – which she is doing now with a vengeance, summoning me repeatedly to Boston – is a race with time. She can't wait until her infant grandsons are grown. She'll leave her collection to her daughters, her taste to me; I'm willing. But I doubt if there's a hurry; her kind are indestructible.

I LIVE WITH WALTER now and have a separate bedroom on the second floor. During the day I work in his office, trying to bring order out of chaos; it's slow going.

"Where is Michelangelo?" he shrieks. "I left him on that chair. Where is he?"

"In a file under 'M,'" I explain.

"I resent this invasion of my privacy. I want to find things where I left them, not off in some silly file you've invented."

"Walter, you asked – even begged – me to create these files. You'd never have found Michelangelo in the papers on that chair. He was under Leonardo and Wordsworth and Aristotle, and a gas bill you still haven't paid. I've put them all in files as you told me to."

"Damn, damn, damn…" he mutters, which is his way of acquiescing.

I sharpen his pencils, clean his pens, keep track of his lecture schedule, and intercept his checks to make sure he deposits them, and his bills to make sure they get paid. Slowly I'm learning when I mustn't distract him from his work, and when I must. The nut huggers are strictly banned during working hours, but not otherwise; I take full advantage.

My reward? Aside from a modest monthly stipend that I intend to negotiate upward, there are lessons in Greek (I'm into Xenophon, will soon read Plato); sudden discourses on art and history that entice me toward dazzling vistas of his Hellas of the mind; nightly visits bringing me the enfolding warmth of a lover, which, now that I know it, I could never again do without; and even, when least expected, sudden capers in his office, where he chases me about and tosses me on the ottoman to ravish me, though the bust of Shakespeare has yet to be toppled. Such is life with America's foremost expounder of Greece and the Renaissance.

He has also promised me a trip to Europe, to view paintings and statuary that he says no reproduction can convey. Since Aunt Jessie has promised me the same, a conflict of the mentors is looming; if they fight over me, I intend to enjoy every minute of it.

With Walter, I feel safer. Even when he's with his family in Hartford, or lecturing in Baltimore or Washington, just knowing him, and knowing he'll be back, I feel safer. Funny thoughts for someone my age, perhaps, but Walter says that in two years I lived twenty.

Sometimes, even with him beside me, I wake up and scream in the night, "I'm scared! I'm scared! I'm scared!"

"Of what? Of whom?" he asks.

"I don't know."

He holds me, calms me. But if alone, I sob myself to sleep.

Somewhere in this city, over on the far East Side amid smells of beer and manure, Contrite sits huddled in his dismal quarters, maybe feeling guilt, maybe not, while lamenting the sorry meanness of his life. But it's not really him I'm afraid of, but *something*. Maybe I'm afraid of night, the night that I was once so eager to explore, the night that broke me. At times I still feel broken; healing is a long, slow thing.

Walter too can sink to the depths. Occasionally I find him in his study, his desk papers swept to the floor, his face buried in his hands.

"Do you realize, Tom, that all I've done is shit? All these lectures, these papers, these books – these grandiose ideas – are shit! They have no meaning, no relevance. It's all just masturbation, a way to kill time. I and everything I've done or hope to do will be flushed away into oblivion, and good riddance – do you hear? – good riddance!"

At these times I don't argue; he might flare up, say savage things. But I mustn't leave him alone. So I sit there quietly, waiting for the mood to subside. Sooner or later it does, and he looks over at me, smiles sheepishly, whispers thanks, and tousles my hair. Then, that night or the next, he will lecture brilliantly on Shakespeare or Sophocles. Tending the ups and downs of this one man is far more challenging and exhausting than ministering to the desires of a hundred. I know; I've done both.

Why did I sleep with all those men? For money? Yes. To get attention? Yes. But also to learn. I wanted to learn about them and myself, and I did. I don't regret any of that, but I'm glad I've left it behind me. Then I was learning with my body; now I'm learning with my mind. To learn is to move on. Neil and Stewart – so different – have the same problem: they're standing still. They're not learning, they're not moving on.

To learn, you have to listen. I like listening to men. I listened to the

Reverend Blythe, then to the Count, and now still more to Walter. I ask only that their talk be interesting; Walter's is fascinating.

Walter thinks I'm eager in too many directions; he wants to focus and discipline my learning. He thinks maybe I should go to college. We'll see; right now I'm busy with his files.

I'm only twenty; I've still got a lot to learn. If someday I have to learn sadness, so be it. If someday I have to learn grief and despair and loneliness, all right. I want to learn. I hope I always will.

Books from Gival Press - Fiction and Nonfiction

Boys, Lost & Found: Storis by Charles Casillo
ISBN: 978-1-928589-33-4, $20.00

Finalist for the 2007 *ForeWord Magazine*'s Book Award for Gay / Lesbian Fiction / Runner up for the 2006 DIY Book Festival Award for Compilations / Anthologies.
"...fascinating, often funny...a safari through the perils and joys of gay life."
—Edward Field

The Cannibal of Guadalajara by David Winner
ISBN: 978-1-928389-50-1, $20.00

Winner of the 2009 Gival Press Novel Award / Honorable Mention 2011 Beach Book Festival Award for Fiction / Finalist National Best Books 2010 Award for Fiction & Literature.
"...a devilishly delicious and disorienting novel. Food, sex, ghastly travel experiences, tantrums, *The Cannibal of Guadalajara* has it all, along with one of the most peculiar versions of the family triad in literary years."
—Joy Williams, a Pulitzer finalist, received the Strauss Living Award from the American Academy of Arts and Letters

A Change of Heart by David Garrett Izzo
ISBN: 978-1-928589-18-1, $20.00

A historical novel about Aldous Huxley and his circle
"astonishingly alive and accurate."
—Roger Lathbury, George Mason University

Dead Time / Tiempo muerto by Carlos Rubio
ISBN: 979-1-928589-17-4, $21.00

Winner of the 2003 Silver Award for Translation, *ForeWord Magazine*'s Book of the Year.
A bilingual (English / Spanish) novel that captures a tale of love and hate, passion and revenge.

Dreams and Other Ailments / Sueños y otros achaques by Teresa Bevin
ISBN: 978-1-92-8589-13-6, $21.00

Winner of the 2001 Bronze Award for Translation, *ForeWord Magazine*'s Book of the Year.
A bilingual (English / Spanish) account of the Latino experience in the USA, filled with humor and hope.

The Gay Herman Melville Reader edited by Ken Schellenberg
ISBN: 978-1-928589-19-8, $16.00

A superb selection of Melville's homoerotic work, with short commentary.

Gone by Sundown by Peter Leach
ISBN: 978-1-928589-61-7, $20.00

Winner of the 2010 Gival Press Novel Award.
"Almost no other novel treats the creation of sundown towns. *Gone by Sundown* thus amounts to a one-volume antidote to American amnesia. On top of that, it's a good read."
—James W. Loewen, author of *Lies My Teacher Told Me* and *Sundown Towns*

An Interdisciplinary Introduction to Women's Studies edited by Brianne Friel & Robert L. Giron
ISBN: 978-1-928589-29-7, $25.00

Winner of the 2005 DIY Book Festival Award for Compilations / Anthologies.
A succinct collection of articles for the college student on a variety of topics.

The Last Day of Paradise by Kiki Denis
ISBN: 978-1-928589-32-7, $20.00

Winner of the 2005 Gival Press Novel Award / Honorable Mention 2007 Hollywood Book Festival.
This debut novel "...is a slippery in-your-face accelerated rush of sex, hokum, and Greek family life."
—Richard Peabody, editor of *Mondo Barbie*

Literatures of the African Diaspora by Yemi D. Ogunyemi
ISBN: 978-1-928589-22-8, $20.00

An important study of the influences in literatures of the world.

Lockjaw: Collected Appalachian Stories by Holly Farris
ISBN: 978-1-928589-38-9, $20.00

Winner of the 2008 Appalachian Writers Association Book of the Year Award for Fiction / Finalist for the 2008 Golden Crown Literary Society Lesbian Short Story / Essay Collections Category / Finalist for the 2008 Eric Hoffler Award for Culture / Finalist for the 2007 Lambda Literary Award for Lesbian Debut Fiction.
"*Lockjaw* sings with all the power of Appalachian storytelling—inventive language, unforgettable voices, narratives that take surprise hairpin turns—without ever romanticizing the region or leaning on stereotypes. Refreshing and passionate, these are stories of unexpected gestures, some brutal, some full of grace, and almost all acts of secret love. A strong and moving collection!"
—Ann Pancake, author of *Given Ground*

Maximus in Catland by David Garrett Izzo
ISBN: 978-1-92-8589-34-1, $20.00

"...*Maximus in Catland* has all the necessary ingredients for a successful fairy tale: good and evil, unrequited love and loving loyalty, heroism and ancient wisdom...."
—Jenny Ivor, author of *Rambles*

Middlebrow Annoyances: American Drama in the 21st Century by Myles Weber
ISBN: 978-1-928589-20-4, $20.00

Current essays on the American theatre scene.

The Pleasuring of Men by Clifford H. Browder
ISBN: 978-1-928589-59-4, $20.00

"...deftly drawn with rich descriptions, a rhythmic balance of action, dialogue, and exposition, and a nicely understated plot. *The Pleasuring of Men* is both engaging and provocative." —Sean Moran

Second Acts by Tim W. Brown
ISBN: 978-1-928589-51-8, $20.00

2011 Runner Up for the New York Book Festival Award for Science Fiction / 2011 Winner of the London Book Festival Award for General Fiction.
"Really clicking, *Second Acts* is a picaresque, sci-fi / western, such as Verne or Welles might have penned it, but with tongue planted firmly in cheek. Tim W. Brown's tale of a husband's search for his fugitive wife takes readers on a whirlwind tour of America, circa 1830. In subverting history Brown's tale celebrates it, with a scholar's eye for authentic details and at a pacing so swift the pages give off a nice breeze."
—Peter Selgin, author of *Life Goes to the Movies*

Secret Memories / Recuerdos secretos by Carlos Rubio
ISBN: 978-1-928589-27-3, $21.00

Finalist for the 2005 *ForeWord Magazine*'s Book of the Year Award for Translations. This bilingual (English / Spanish) novel adeptly pulls the reader into the world of the narrator who is vulnerable.

Show Up, Look Good by Mark Wisniewski
ISBN: 978-1-928589-60-0, $20.00

Finalist for the 2009 Gival Press Novel Award.
"..a rollicking, laugh-out-loud romp of a novel, a picaresque spin through fin-de-siècle New York as seen through the eyes of its intrepid, Midwestern-born heroine...."—Ben Fountain, author of *Brief Encounters with Che Guevara*
"Wisniewski: a riotously original voice."—Jonathan Lethem

The Smoke Week: Sept. 11-21, 2001 by Ellis Avery
ISBN: 978-1-928589-24-2, $15.00

2004 *Writer's Notes Magazine* Book Award—Notable for Culture / Winner of the Ohionana Library Walter Rumsey Marvin Award. "Here is Witness. Here is Testimony."
—Maxine Hong Kingston, author of *The Fifth Book of Peace*

The Spanish Teacher by Barbara de la Cuesta
ISBN: 978-1-928589-37-2, $20.00

Winner of the 2006 Gival Press Novel Award / Finalist for the 2007 *ForeWord Magazine*'s Book of the Year / Award for Fiction-General / Honorable Mention for the 2007 London Book Festival. "...De la Cuesta's novel maintains an accumulating power which holds onto a reader's attention not only through the forceful figure of Ordóñez, but by demonstrating acutely how ordinary lives are impacted by the underlying social and political landscape. Compelling reading."—Tom Tolnay, author of *Selling America* and *This is the Forest Primeval*

That Demon Life by Lowell Mick White
ISBN: 978-1-928589-47-1, $21.00

Winner of the 2008 Gival Press Novel Award / Finalist for the 2010 Texas Book Award for Fiction / Finalist for the 2009 National / Best Book Award for Fiction.
"*That Demon Life* is a hoot, a virtuoso tale by a master story teller."
—Larry Heinermann, author of *Paco's Story*, winner of the National Book Award

Tina Springs into Summer / Tina se lanza al verano by Teresa Bevin
ISBN: 978-1-928589-28-0, $21.00

2006 *Writer's Notes Magazine* Book Award—Notable for Young Adult Literature. A bilingual (English / Spanish) compelling story of a youngster from a multi-cultural urban setting and her urgency to fit in.

A Tomb on the Periphery by John Domini
ISBN: 978-1-928589-40-2, $20.00

Honorable Mention for the 2009 London Book Festival Award for Fiction / Finalist for the 2005 Gival Press Novel Award.
"Stolen antiquities, small-time thugs, a sultry femme fatale.... a book that takes the trappings of noir then transcends the genre...." *Bookslut*

Twelve Rivers of the Body by Elizabeth Oness

ISBN: 978-1-928589-44-0, $20.00

Winner of the 2007 Gival Press Novel Award
"*Twelve Rivers of the Body* lyrically evokes downtown Washington, DC in the 1980s, before the real estate boom, before gentrification, as the city limped from one crisis to another—crack addiction, AIDS, a crumbling infrastructure. This beautifully evoked novel traces Elena's imperfect struggle, like her adopted city's, to find wholeness and healing."
—Kim Roberts, author of *The Kimnama*

For a complete list of titles, visit: *www.givalpress.com.*
Books available via Ingram, the Internet, and other outlets.

Or Write:

Gival Press, LLC
PO Box 3812
Arlington, VA 22203
703.351.0079

www.ingramcontent.com/pod-product-compliance
Lightning Source LLC
Chambersburg PA
CBHW030247030726
47493CB00023B/1061